BEAR TOWNE UNIVERSITY

STUDENT HANDBOOK

BEAR TOWNE UNIVERSITY

STUDENT HANDBOOK

A Companion Guide to EERIE

By C.M. McCoy

Adventure Write (Publisher)
Wasilla, Alaska 99654 www.adventurewrite.com

First Adventure Write trade paperback edition, April 2026

This is a work of fiction. The characters, organizations, and events in this book are fictitious. Any similarity to real persons, living or dead, is coincidental and not intended by the author.

Library of Congress Control Number: 2026906136
Library of Congress Cataloging-in-Publication Data C.M. McCoy.
McCoy, C. M.
Bear Towne University Student Handbook / C. M. McCoy.

ISBN: 979-8-9932605-5-6 (Paperback, Amazon)
ISBN: 979-8-9932605-6-3 (Paperback, IngramSpark)

1. Universities and colleges — Fiction. 2. Student handbooks — Fiction. 3. Campus life — Fiction. 4. Paranormal — Fiction. 5. Alaska — Fiction.
I. Title
10 9 8 7 6 5 4 3 2 1

Cover Art & Interior Art by Colleen Oefelein and Adventure Write
Cover Design & Book Design by Adventure Write

Printed in the United States of America

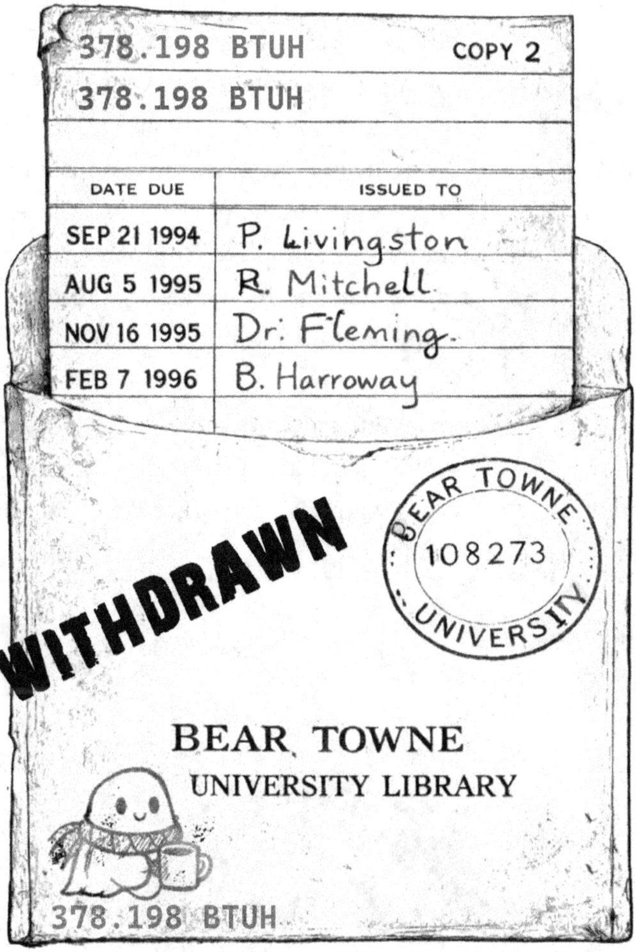
378.198 BTUH COPY 2
378.198 BTUH
DATE DUE
ISSUED TO
SEP 21 1994 P. Livingston
AUG 5 1995 R. Mitchell
NOV 16 1995 Dr. Fleming
FEB 7 1996 B. Harroway
WITHDRAWN
BEAR TOWNE
108273
UNIVERSITY
BEAR TOWNE
UNIVERSITY LIBRARY
378.198 BTUH

A WARNING

Welcome to Bear Towne, a place of learning carved out of wild country, where scholarship and survival go hand in hand. Hear this well: This is not a refuge for malice. Those who think to bring violence, dark rites, or willful corruption of others onto our grounds will find themselves

removed — decisively and without favor. Bear Towne protects its own. We will not hesitate to expel, detain, or otherwise neutralize threats to the life and study of this community. That protection extends to every soul here, human and non-human alike. You will not endanger the fragile balance that makes this university both unique and survivable.

Carry our motto with you — *Deo Confide, Timere Nihil.* Work hard, learn humbly, respect the others on campus, and tend to your soul. Do otherwise, and you will quickly learn what pain means.

Asher the Benevolent
President, Bear Towne University

WELCOME

It is my great honor to welcome you to Bear Towne University, where knowledge and character are forged in equal measure. You have chosen to join a rare community of scholars and athletes, dreamers and technicians, and yes, others whose origins you may not find recorded in

any enrollment registry. We acknowledge our differences, but we celebrate our commonalities, because that is what bolsters intellect with integrity and tempers arrogance with humility.

Here, nestled in the heart of Alaska, you will find not only rigorous study and spirited debate, but also the enduring bonds of fellowship that transform classmates into lifelong allies. Whether your path leads you through the sciences, the arts, or the mysteries that lie between, our faculty and staff are committed to guiding you with wisdom, compassion, and a touch of severity befitting life in the Great White North.

We admit only the highest achievers here. Only the most resilient complete the requirements for a degree in ParaScience. At Bear Towne, you will sit shoulder to shoulder with peers whose lives may seem unfamiliar, perhaps even otherworldly, but it is precisely this breadth of perspective that drives innovation and shapes our students into leaders of rare understanding and courage.

May you face your studies and your future with confidence, knowing you are part of a tradition that has endured over 800 years. Welcome to Bear Towne University. Your journey begins now.

Trust God and fear nothing,
Dr. Simeon Woodfork, M.D., J.D., PhD.
University V.P. and Dean of the College of ParaScience

TABLE OF CONTENTS

CHINOOK
HALL

I. GETTING TO CAMPUS

A UNIQUE EXPERIENCE

Your journey to Bear Towne University in The Middle of Nowhere, Alaska will be one you won't soon forget. More of an adventure than a flight, an "excursion" on the Luftzeug/*Traumzeug* is the world's most exclusive and sought-after extreme activity, topping Mortimer's List of Adrenaline Junkie Thrills for more than 25 years.

Buckle up! This is no ordinary airplane! Following your flight, you will join the ranks of brave explorers who've conquered liminal travel before you. The list of successful *Traumzeugers* includes remarkable explorers who have gone on to become astronauts, moon walkers, and even Nobel Prize-winning researchers.

Approximately three hours prior to your landing in Alaska, the aircraft will undergo its change from Luftzeug to *Traumzeug*, and your first course in ParaScience will begin. Students should not panic.

THE LUFTZEUG/TRAUMZEUG: YOUR FLIGHT TO ALASKA

The Luftzeug/*Traumzeug* is both an air tool (Luftzeug) and a dream tool (*Traumzeug*). There is no way to mentally prepare for this flight.

This is not a commercial flight; this is a research flight. Students will do well to remember these tips:

- Do not approach the flight crew. The flight crew are not traditional flight attendants, and they are not trained in hospitality. Nor are they friendly. They have one job, and that is to load and operate the Luftzeug/*Traumzeug*. They will deliver you, alive, through the airspace and dreamspace and into The Middle of Nowhere.

- Avoid the flight crew. Some may be ill-tempered and react impolitely.

PREPARING FOR YOUR FLIGHT

All incoming ParaScience freshmen are REQUIRED to complete their journey to the university via Luftzeug and attend **ParaScience 101, An Introduction**, which is a 3-credit course conducted on board. You are advised not to panic and to hold all questions until your arrival on campus.

Flights depart from Frankfurt, Moscow, and Pittsburgh approximately one week prior to the start of the semester. Your Bear Towne University welcome packet will arrive to you in the mail and contain your personal travel itinerary and transportation instructions.

You MUST collect your boarding pass from the Bear Towne kiosk at your departure airport, personally, to receive your initiation charge. Finally, do not stare at your fellow passengers.

WHAT TO PACK: YOUR CARRY-ON

The Luftzeug can be quite drafty, and passengers should wear or bring warm clothing and sturdy shoes. Ear and eye protection are available on board under your seat, with the activation switch located in the button bank above each seat. Life jackets will be provided.

We're proud to offer our freshmen a choice of boxed meals, tailored to their digestive needs. Hot coffee and tea as well as water and Ooze are available at the self-service galley throughout the flight.

There are no restrictions on the size, weight, or number of your carry-on items, and no restrictions on liquids. Students may bring their own food and drink as long as that food or drink is not the product of the slaughter of a human or human-looking non-human.

Bear in mind you may have the opportunity to collect your carry-on items when you disembark. Rest assured any items abandoned on board will be returned to you with your checked baggage.

Students should pack the following WITH their carry-on items:
- Ground pad, sleeping bag, and pillow
- Large towel or robe
- Dry change of clothes
- Spare shoes
- Washing cloth and bar of soap

WHAT TO PACK: YOUR CHECKED BAGGAGE

PERCUSSIVE INSTRUMENTS ARE FORBIDDEN at BTU.

All students must pack for interior Alaska's harsh winter climate and for BTU's unique and remote environment. Though many items are available for sale at the Bear Towne bookstore, it isn't Walmart. (The closest Walmart is, in good weather, a 4-hour drive, and the closest Strommhof is in Washington State.)

Standard dormitory rooms come furnished with a bed and bare mattress, a desk and chair, a wardrobe, and a small trash can, as well as ceiling zips, an Indispensable™ Ghost Trap, and all-winter light. Dormitories feature shared bathrooms, laundry rooms, rotary telephones, and a kitchenette on each floor.

We recommend students bring the following:

Dormitory Items
- Bedding: pillow, sheets, and blankets
- Shower supplies: bathrobe, slippers, towels
- Toiletries: toothbrush and paste, soaps, lotions, hairbrush
- School supplies: notebooks, paper, ink, pens, and pencils
- Appliances: alarm clock, hairdryer, boombox (with headphones), typewriter or computer/printer

A typical dorm room

   © 1210 Bear Towne University | The Middle Of Nowhere, Alaska

Electronics

Do note that while BTU now offers full electricity, water, and a telephone nook in all dormitories, it remains "off-grid" insofar as it enjoys neither cellular nor Wi-Fi service nor internet service of any kind outside of the library. Bring a watch.

Personal Items

- Clothes: daily wear, formal wear, swimsuit, fuzzy robe, slippers
- Earplugs/Buzzdoodles, water bottle, coffee mug, beauty and laundry supplies
- Shoes: sneakers, hiking boots, wellies, snow boots, formal shoes
- Coats: parka, insulative coat, rain coat, windbreaker

Winter Gear

Remember: there's no such thing as cold weather, just inappropriate clothing. Temperatures on campus can reach negative 40 degrees Fahrenheit. And then there's the wind.

All ParaScience freshmen will make a winter-weather foray into the White Forest. To reduce the risk of a stay at Bear Towne University Hospital (see pg 60, "BTU Hospital" in "Section VIII: Campus Hazards and Peculiarities"), students must bring appropriate gear:

- Snow boots/warm socks
- Parka/snow pants/snowsuit
- Snow skirt/hats/scarf/balaclava
- Clothes that layer well
- Headlamp/goggles
- Hats/gloves/mittens/liners
- Hand warmers/foot warmers/body warmers

Recreation Gea

Bear Towne University offers great star-gazing, bird-watching, daytime tree-spotting, nighttime Aurora gazing, hiking trails, campsites, mountain biking trails, Alpine ski slopes, groomed cross country trails, skate-ski trails, backcountry skiing, ski-mountaineering, fat-tire biking trails, outdoor ice rinks, an indoor ice complex, and a swimming pool.

Students may bring:
- Bicycles
- Magnoggles
- Skis (all the skis)
- Ice skates
- Hockey gear
- Hiking gear
- Camping gear

Above all, students should bring an open mind, a spirit of adventure, and a healthy supply of patience.

II. ARRIVING ON CAMPUS

WHAT TO EXPECT DURING YOUR FLIGHT

There is no way to mentally prepare for a flight on board the Luftzeug/*Traumzeug*, except to remind oneself of two things:

1. Keep an open mind (don't panic)
2. Don't panic

Approximately five minutes before the flight crew initiates *Traumzeug* operations and floods the cabin with sleeping gas, a violet light will illuminate. This is your signal to prepare and enter your sleeping bag.

"LANDING" AT BEAR TOWNE

Luftzeug operators strive to deliver students to the landing zone just south of Bear Towne University's main campus, however, some deviation is to be expected, and students should prepare for a short hike through questionable terrain after touching down.

In case of a projected water landing, our Luftzeug crew will distribute life jackets prior to dropping you out.

For safety, students should stick together during the hike to campus.

Once on campus, students should report to Chinook Hall for recovery. See the map on the following page.

THE MIDDLE OF NOWHERE, ALASKA
BEAR TOWNE UNIVERSITY
Cold Lake
LANDING ZONE

III. CAMPUS RULES (AND PUNISHMENTS)

Bear Towne University is committed to providing a rigorous academic environment in a geographically and metaphysically complex region. Student safety is a shared responsibility. Compliance with the following guidelines is mandatory.

Failure to adhere to university advisories may result in injury, relocation, extraction, confinement, or other corrective measures.

A. INTERPERSONAL CONDUCT

1. Restricted Associations

Students may be advised—formally or informally—to limit or avoid contact with specific individuals for reasons of safety. Such advisories are issued in the interest of community welfare or bodily integrity and are not subject to debate.

2. Enforcement of Directives

Bear Towne University does not guarantee repeated warnings. Students are expected to remember and comply with instructions as given.

B. ADMINISTRATIVE AUTHORITY

3. Documentation Supremacy

Official university documentation remains authoritative even when student experience appears to contradict it.

4. Outcome-Based Compliance

Survival and continued enrollment constitute evidence of compliance.

C. FINAL NOTICE

Bear Towne University does not eliminate risk. It manages it.

Students unwilling to accept this are encouraged to reconsider enrollment at BTU.

Avoid volatile students.

Never stare at a non-human, as some find this behavior threatening.

The President's residence, gardens, and observatory are off-limits to students.

When you witness a student punishment, take note of the offense and avoid making the same mistake.

Humans from Outside should travel through the White Forest only when escorted by a non-human.

Always carry yeti spray and cross your fingers when venturing into the White Forest. *spray doesn't work when it's raining!*

Get to know the active in-betweens, and avoid the unknown ones.

Ready your in-between extraction technique. *Yeah....THEY NEVER TAUGHT US ONE*

Above all: tend to your soul. *HOW?*

IV. BEAR TOWNE CULTURE

At Bear Towne University, tradition is carefully preserved, history is meticulously recorded, and nothing important has ever truly been lost.

At BTU, generations of students have built a rich culture of curiosity, resilience, and adaptation—qualities that remain essential to campus life today.

Life at Bear Towne is shaped as much by routine as by anomaly. Students attend lectures in buildings that predate their blueprints, learn ParaScience alongside traditional coursework, and quickly discover that certain shortcuts, tunnels, and gathering places are best used selectively. Campus culture prizes adaptability, dark humor, and an unspoken respect for rules that are not always written down.

Historically, the university has responded to unusual events with documentation rather than alarm.

Incidents are classified; hazards are stabilized when possible, and when they are not, our residents simply adjust. Over time, this approach has produced a student body fluent in both scholarship and survival, one that understands when to ask questions and just as importantly, when to duck and cover.

Familiarity with the university's past will not prevent surprises, but it may help you better adjust to living on the edge of comfort.

Since 1210, the mission of Bear Towne University is to pierce the Veil.

OUR HISTORY

Bear Towne University was founded to study phenomena most institutions refuse to acknowledge. Its history is marked by ambitious research, catastrophic failure, and a long institutional shift from reckless exploration to careful containment. Rather than erasing its past, the university has absorbed it into daily campus life, producing a culture that prizes discretion and survival over reassurance.

BEAR TOWNE UNIVERSITY

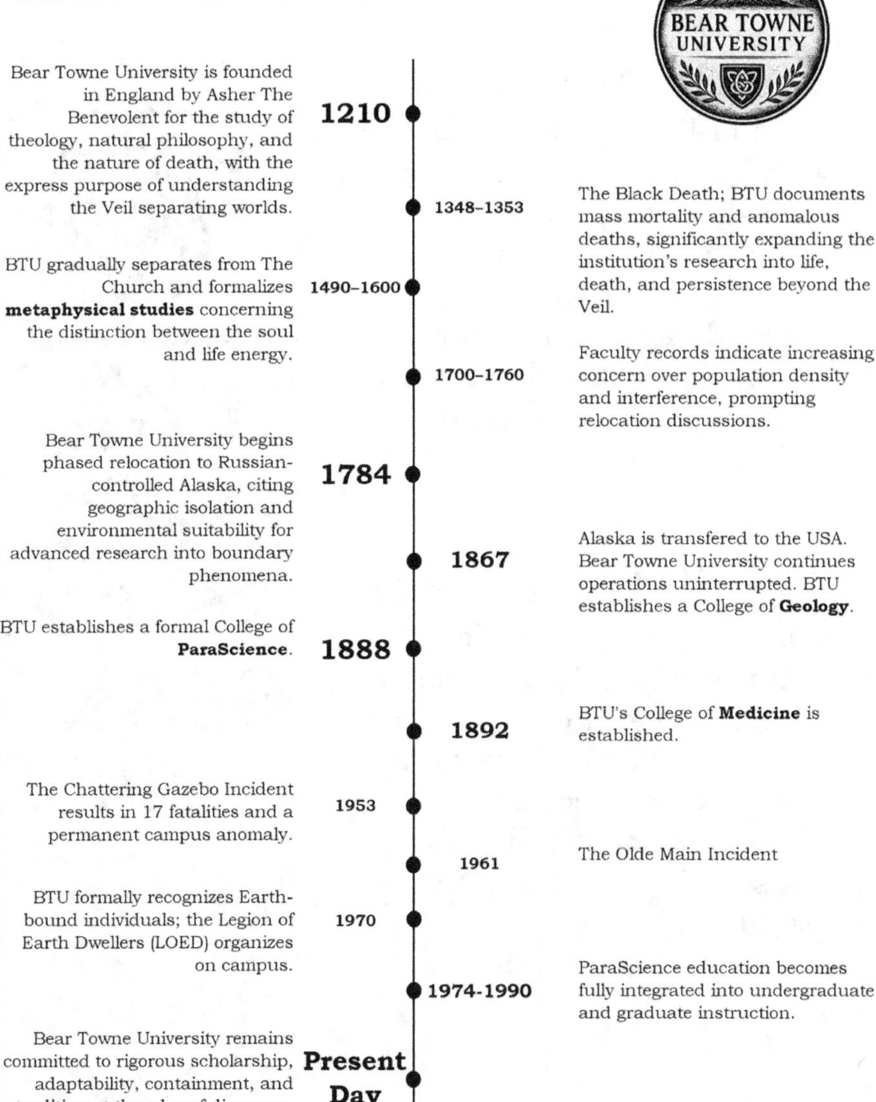

1210 — Bear Towne University is founded in England by Asher The Benevolent for the study of theology, natural philosophy, and the nature of death, with the express purpose of understanding the Veil separating worlds.

1348–1353 — The Black Death; BTU documents mass mortality and anomalous deaths, significantly expanding the institution's research into life, death, and persistence beyond the Veil.

1490–1600 — BTU gradually separates from The Church and formalizes **metaphysical studies** concerning the distinction between the soul and life energy.

1700–1760 — Faculty records indicate increasing concern over population density and interference, prompting relocation discussions.

1784 — Bear Towne University begins phased relocation to Russian-controlled Alaska, citing geographic isolation and environmental suitability for advanced research into boundary phenomena.

1867 — Alaska is transfered to the USA. Bear Towne University continues operations uninterrupted. BTU establishes a College of **Geology**.

1888 — BTU establishes a formal College of **ParaScience**.

1892 — BTU's College of **Medicine** is established.

1953 — The Chattering Gazebo Incident results in 17 fatalities and a permanent campus anomaly.

1961 — The Olde Main Incident

1970 — BTU formally recognizes Earth-bound individuals; the Legion of Earth Dwellers (LOED) organizes on campus.

1974-1990 — ParaScience education becomes fully integrated into undergraduate and graduate instruction.

Present Day — Bear Towne University remains committed to rigorous scholarship, adaptability, containment, and tradition at the edge of discovery.

The Bear represents the spirit of BTU students: they're weirdly curious walking tanks with sharp teeth, long memories, and fierce opinions. It reminds students that survival here is not about dominance, but understanding when to stand firm and when to give ground.

The Yeti represents the warrior spirit, respect for nature, and the human/non-human cooperation that exists at Bear Towne University. In 1954, the Yeti became the official mascot of BTU, and Yetis hockey was formally established.

Ursa Major "The Great Bear" constellation and the North Star (Polaris) signify navigation. The deliberately imprecise stars honor BTU's home in Alaska and reminds students to look up when the ground beneath them can no longer be trusted.

The Alpha and Omega symbolize beginnings and endings and reflect BTU's foundational devotion with the Veil: where life starts, where it ends, and what happens when those boundaries fail.

HIDING IN PLAIN SIGHT (NOBODY WILL BELIEVE YOU)

Think you're going to get a picture of a furry yeti in the White Forest and show all your friends back home? Think again.

Most of the unusual things you see at Bear Towne University are camouflaged, so to speak, and your human friends likely won't see them.

How, you ask? Well, the human brain has a natural tendency to filter out what it cannot safely categorize. So, a poltergeist in the attic may move your great-gramma's trunk around at night, but you'll never see it. Just like you never realized your hairy neighbor who loves wearing green is actually a Leprechaun. In fact, without an initiation charge, you likely wouldn't perceive the paranormal on campus either. Most paranormal beings, objects, and phenomena don't have to conceal themselves to blend in. They know most people won't see Aethereal creatures or boundary events clearly—even when they are directly in front of them—because the mind edits the experience into something acceptable.

Once you get your initiation charge, that natural cognitive protection goes bye-bye. Your brain is irreversibly and forever altered—the "Aethereal camo" is removed, and you will see creatures and phenomena as they truly are.

This is why visitors and family members "back home" won't believe you when you describe a zinging bookworm, even if you have the pictures to prove it. Pro tip: save yourself the strange looks and ridicule, and talk about the food instead.

THE SPIRIT OF THE YETI

Bear Towne University did not choose the yeti as its mascot because it is safe, friendly, or particularly invested in student retention.

It is none of those.

The yeti is:
Strong
Hungry
Ferocious
Loyal
Clever
(in that order)

What better symbol could there be for us! At Bear Towne, the yeti is more than a mascot. It is our hockey team and our campus symbol. It is our students: mud-splattered, sleep-deprived, and stubbornly surviving. And, most importantly, it is our neighbor in the White Forest.

The Yetis take their name from the same half-mythic creature that has been spotted (and occasionally collided with) along campus trails for generations.

And yes, while the yeti is likely responsible for several injuries, a handful of disappearances, and at least one deeply regrettable premature death, Bear Towne believes tradition matters. Besides, if you can learn to coexist with a yeti, you can learn to coexist with anything.

Including your roommate.

BTU

YETIS HOCKEY AT BTU

Let's be honest.

We built a university on a thin seam between realms, and somehow the most intense thing on campus is still our hockey team.

The Yetis are not "spirited." They are not "enthusiastic."

They are a full-campus personality disorder on ice.

Students from every college—including the ones who claim they "don't do sports"—will scream themselves hoarse. The same person who calmly leads excursions into temporary in-betweens will absolutely lose their scat over a missed power play.

Our Reputation
Other teams describe playing the Yetis as physically demanding, emotionally destabilizing, and the absolute toughest game of their year.

We forecheck like we've lost our grant funding.
We body-check like we're correcting a historical injustice.
We celebrate like we personally fractured the barrier!

Away Games
BTU provides student transportation to away games. The buses are full, freezing, and loud.

Bring layers, bring snacks, and bring your voice. But leave your dignity behind.

BTU Alma Mater

Break down the Barrier,
Build up the Ferrier,
You breathe in the eerie air,
Pierce the veil. Pierce the veil.

When first the veil was torn,
By mortal will and scorn,
A brighter path was born,
Through the veil. Through the veil.

When barrier first fell
The ferry men knew well
What silence would not tell
Through the veil! Through the veil!

They saw the seam laid bare
And chose to enter there
Though warned not to dare
Hold the breach! Hold the breach!

What mortal hands began
We finish if we can
And walk the breach again
Envoy home! Envoy home!

From breach our banner flies,
Where hidden knowledge lies,
And none but brave denies,
Stand and sing! Stand and sing!

Where fracture first was made,
Our legacy was laid,
And still we're unafraid,
Pierce the veil. Pierce the veil.

A legacy of light,
Benevolence is right,
For righteousness we fight,
Old Towne we hail. Old Towne we hail!

   © 1210 Bear Towne University | The Middle Of Nowhere, Alaska

V. ACADEMIC PROGRAMS

NOTE: Undergraduate students may transfer colleges and change majors through their sophomore year without affecting their graduation date.

THE COLLEGE OF PARASCIENCE: THE FOUNDATION OF THE UNIVERSITY

ParaScience: where "unexplained" is a temporary classification.

Bear Towne University's College of ParaScience is the world's oldest and largest institution devoted to the study of Aethereal phenomena.

Renowned for its research into astrophysics, philosophy, new technologies, and weaponry, it remains a premier paranormal laboratory: half scholarly devotion and half controlled hazard zone.

Ambitious research sometimes means catastrophic failure, but we're proud that we've evolved from reckless exploration to careful containment.

ParaScience students can expect rigorous training in interstitial physics, boundary theory, classification systems, and field documentation; and practice in studying phenomena that respond poorly to being observed. Our faculty are proud to support fearless minds, steady hands, and students who can follow directions.

Your first BTU class is ParaScience 110 — An Explanation of Strange, a fun 4-credit exploratory course presented aboard the *Traumzeug* that explains why this university exists and demonstrates how to survive here.

Remember: the paranormal isn't rare. It's just inconvenient. It may be terrifying, but at least it's measurable.

THE COLLEGE OF MEDICINE AND PARAMEDICINE
CARE FOR ALL CREATURES

As we're the world's only university using Aethereal Science in medical research and training, our students have been at the tip-of-the-spear in emerging treatments. From the laboratory to the battlefield and bedside, BTU's medical graduates set the standard of human and non-human care for the world.

BTU's College of Medicine students can expect rigorous coursework in anatomy, physiology, pharmacology, and emergency medicine, alongside specialized instruction in soul-tending, venom response, trauma stabilization under anomalous conditions, and the subtle art of treating a patient who is technically not "alive."

Not a Med Student? Consider a ParaMed elective! It may just save your life!

Not everyone at Bear Towne University studies medicine— but everyone here benefits from knowing how to stop the bleeding, treat shock, and stabilize a friend who got too curious in the White Forest.

Intro to ParaMedicine, a wildly popular 4-credit exploratory course, is designed specifically for non-med majors. You'll learn the basics of first aid, triage, and emergency response, with special attention to the kinds of injuries that occur when you attend a university built on the edge of the Veil.

Rock paper scissors—dig! Bear Towne University's undergraduate program in Geology is for dirt lovers, treasure hunters, and rock hounds. From tiny rock hammers to proper pickaxes, backhoes and excavators, our students learn not only the Aethereal aspect of Earth Science in Alaska, but also the practical operation of heavy equipment and tools many universities find beneath them.

The Geology program at BTU requires several extended off-campus field trips which involve moderate to strenuous outdoor activity (e.g. all-day field exercises, digs, and hiking), including a 5-week capstone expedition and excavation to the Brooks Range in the Halls of the Mountain Ring.

For students enrolled in one of our other colleges, the Geology department offers Geology 101 — Rocks for People Who Think They Hate Rocks, a fun 4-credit class that unearths the fundamentals of interstitial mineral formation, anomalous fault lines, and the long-standing question of why certain stones "remember." Roll up your sleeves, throw on a hard hat and join us!

VI. STUDENT SERVICES

I-MET

I-MET handles BTU's security, search & rescue, emergency services, student transportation, interstitial travel, mail delivery, device repairs, and maintenance. They care for our university facilities and family with the security and emotional warmth of a shrink-wrapped pallet.

Q: What is I-MET?
A: I-MET is Bear Towne University's Interstitial Maintenance & Emergency Team. They're in charge of: emergency medical services, fire suppression, Luftzeug service, in-between extractions, structural inspections, hazard stabilization, and campus investigations.
They perform all of these tasks efficiently and without emotional engagement.

Q: Are I-MET members human?
A: Some of them used to be.

Q: Why do they wear gray flight suits?
A: Some wear maroon ones. They have a lot of pockets, and we hear they're quite comfortable.

Q: Why do they always cover their faces?
A: To avoid causing a panic.

Q: Do they always wear gas masks?
A: No. Sometimes it's a full-face respirator and sometimes it's an item best described as "theatrical."

Q: Why do they march everywhere?
A: As far as we can tell, they do this for two reasons: to project good order and discipline, and to discourage conversation.

Q: I saw one standing in a weird position. Is it injured?
A: No. I-MET cannot be injured.

Q: Do I call 911 if I need an ambulance or firetruck?
A: No. I-MET will know if their services are needed and simply
show up.

Q: How do they know to show up?
A: All zombies are on the clairvoyant spectrum, which is why
I-MET runs campus emergency services and SAR.

Q: I saw one leaning unnaturally. How do they do that?
A: They're big fans of Michael Jackson.

Q: I-MET took my luggage. Will I get it back?
A: Yes. Probably.

Q: When?
A: When they bring it to you.

Q: Why do they shrink-wrap our luggage on the Luftzeug?
A: To keep it from falling out of the Luftzeug or tumbling onto a student and crushing them to death.

Q: I heard they inspect the Luftzeug rivet by rivet. Why do they do that?
A: A loose rivet caused the 1971 loss of an entire freshman ParaScience class (most of the class were recovered in 1975). BTU strongly prefers to never repeat that mishap.

Q: What should I do if I-MET approaches me?
A: 1. Don't panic.
    2. Be still.
    3. Keep your hands visible.
    4. Answer only what is asked.
    5. Follow their orders.
    6. Do not make jokes—I-MET takes everything literally.
    7. Do not ask for clarification.
    8. Do not ask where they're taking you.
    9. Do not ask anything.

Q: What happens if I do ask a question?
A: Nothing good.

Q: Can I join I-MET?
A: Short answer: no. One does not "join" I-MET. One may be conscripted to serve, but that process is opaque. I-MET is an elite force. It recruits only unalive, animated former "beings" into its workforce. I-MET does not accept applications.

Q: What's that smell?
A: I-MET does emit an odor some describe as a mix of antiseptic and pennies. That is the smell of safety.

Q: Does I-MET have names?
A: Sort of, but don't try to pronounce them. Just use, "Sir."

Q: Do I-MET members sleep?
A: Yes, but not like a fully alive human.

Q: Can I thank I-MET if they help me?
A: Yes. Most students report their gratitude was met with an uncomfortable pause, a long stare, and a hiss.

Q: I-MET took my roommate, and I haven't seen him in a week now. Should I be concerned?
A: Yes. Check the BTU hospital.

BEAR TOWNE UNIVERSITY HOSPITAL

Fun fact: More than 50% of BTU students receive life-saving care at Bear Towne University Hospital before they graduate, and 90% of freshmen seek treatment for a range of complaints before the end of their first semester.

Bottom line: you'll likely use BTU Hospital. So let's get acquainted.

Given the age and nature of our university, coupled with the sheer number of hazards on campus, it's no surprise that Bear Towne University Hospital (BTUH) has evolved into a world-renowned trauma center, as well as the world's only facility equipped to treat Aethereal conditions and injuries.

Be aware that BTUH is a teaching hospital, and mistakes do happen. But that shouldn't deter you from seeking care! Don't believe all the rumors you hear. Some of the more dramatic incident reports have been greatly exaggerated over the decades. There have only been a handful of flesh-eating zombitis infections of late, and our resident banshee has greatly improved her bedside manner.*

It is worth noting that the Aethereal wing at BTUH is also a medical research center, where emerging treatments and remedies are perfected (with the help of our student patients, of course).

All in all, BTUH is equipped to handle everything from simple colds, cuts, and bruises, to major limb reattachments, oneiric entrapment (REM-lock), and even minor soul regeneration.

With so much innovation and cutting-edge research, it stands to reason that as BTUH treats humans and non-humans from across the globe, students can expect to see things in our hallways they've never dreamed of (and some they have).

See pg 60, "BTU Hospital" in "Section VIII: Campus Hazards and Peculiarities."

   © 1210 Bear Towne University | The Middle Of Nowhere, Alaska

As one physician famously put it:

"Were it not for our reckless students who find new and creative
ways to injure themselves, we'd be a normal hospital."

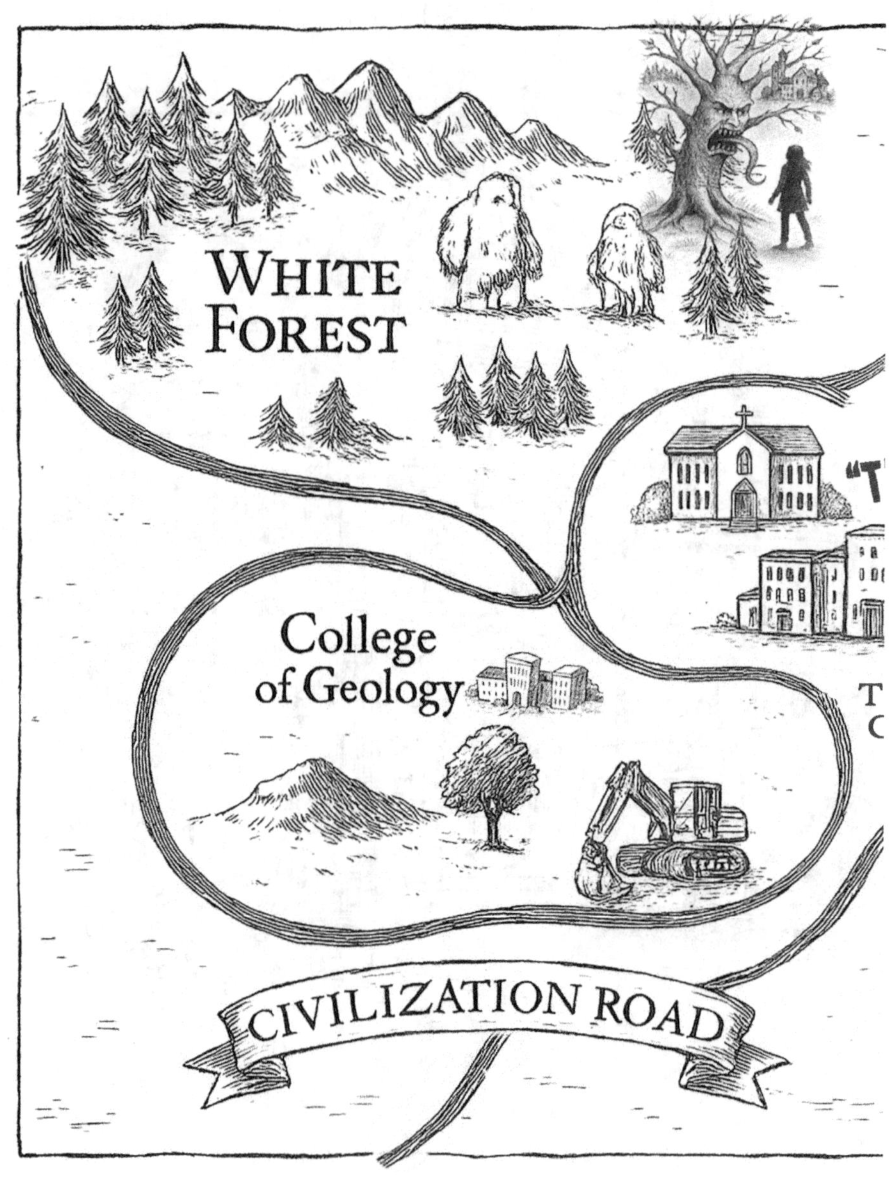

WHITE FOREST
College of Geology
CIVILIZATION ROAD

Olde Main
College of ParaScience
IGLOO ARENA
Edge Labs
President's Residence
"THE BOWL"
Trinity Center
Eureka Hall
Library
Hospital
College of Pre-Medicine
Bear Towne University

VII. RESIDENCE LIFE

DORMITORIES

Your Practical Guide to Staying Fed and Rested (and Out of the Incident Reports)

Student life here in Alaska can be anything from the most amazing time of your life to fatal. But BTU has designed its campus to really minimize the instances of preventable premature student deaths.

Whether you're settling into your dorm room, navigating your first cafeteria meal, or hauling your gear to the arena, you'll find that BTU provides everything a student needs: a bed, a warm meal, and at least one structured way to release stress before it turns into poor decision-making.

HOUSING: EUREKA HALL & RESIDENT LIFE

Most freshmen ParaScience students lodge in Eureka Hall, the university's only co-ed dormitory.

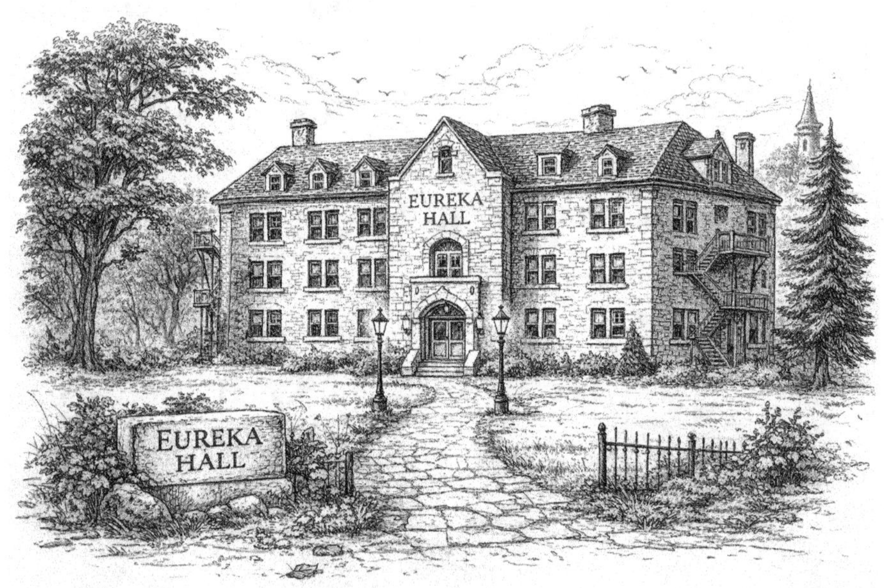

BTU 1981

The building is organized with gents' rooms in the east wing and ladies' rooms in the west wing, with each wing featuring shared facilities such as showers, laundry. Each floor also offers a multi-use common area serving as a study hall, TV and game room, and kitchenette.

A Resident Assistant suite is located on each floor near the common area. If you need help, go to your R.A. first.

Every dormitory at BTU has a piano room on the ground floor.

Incoming students should pick up a standard welcome package upon arrival, which includes essentials such as a campus map, yeti spray, and fuel for your dormitory room **ghost trap** (see below). Fuel your trap and do not remove it.

POLTERGEISTS IN THE DORMS

If you experience a poltergeist event, do not attempt to communicate, bargain with, insult, or challenge it. Fuel your ghost trap as directed, keep your room tidy, and report sustained activity to your R.A., especially if the poltergeist responds to your emotions, arranges objects into geometric shapes, or demonstrates a sense of humor. These are troubling signs of an evolving geist.

Remember: most poltergeists are not malicious; they are simply bored, territorial, and extremely invested in freshman angst.

GOOD FOOD: CHINOOK HALL

Affectionately called "The Trough," Chinook Hall is where you'll find breakfast, lunch, and dinner (served on plates).

Meals are cafeteria-style: grab a tray, move with the line, sit wherever you can find a seat, eat your food, and leave.

Location: The Bowl (the area at the center of campus)

Hours
Breakfast:
Mon-Fri 0500-0830
Sat-Sun Brunch 0500-1100

Lunch:
Mon-Fri 1000-1300

Dinner:
Daily 1600-1830

Features:
Fruit and salad bar
Hot food buffet
Non-human buffet*
Soup of the day
Fresh-baked bread
Grab-and-go sandwiches, burgers, and pizza
Ice cream and dessert bar

* Note to our human students: One of the surest ways to earn a helping hand from I-MET and a free trip to Bear Towne University hospital is to eat from the non-human buffet. It is not adventurous; it's just dumb.

Most students find the chow hall comforting in the same way they find a laundry room comforting: it's familiar, functional, loud, and statistically less likely to kill you than the White Forest.

Bon appétit!

BETTER FOOD: THE BRUISED MOOSE CAFÉ

The Bruised Moose offers pizza, burgers, and grilled sandwiches 24/7 along with a variety of drinks and comfort foods for humans and non-humans alike. There is a barista on staff during waking hours who prepares not only artisan coffees and smoothies, but also makes our campus famous for the perfect cup of hot Ooze—a favorite of our non-humans (also safe for human consumption, but we don't recommend it).

Location: The Bowl inside Trinity Square

Hours: Always open

Freshman Tip: Get to know the grill master, Mitch. He's been the head chef at The Bruised Moose since it opened in 1852. Ask him for a reindeer cheesesteak.

FITNESS: THE TRINITY CENTER'S "REC HALL"

Rec Hall at Trinity Center in The Bowl is where you'll find everything you need to stay fit, blow off some steam, or have some craic.

Hours
  Daily 0500-2400

Features:
  Basketball courts
  Pickleball courts
  Indoor running track
  Indoor field (soccer, Kubb, badminton, etc)
  White Forest confidence course
  Weight center
  Yoga room
  Arcade
  Pool tables / Darts / Ping Pong
  Outdoor rec equipment sign-out: bikes, sleds, skis, fishing equipment, snowshoes, snowmachines, ATVs, etc.

Each college and most dorms pull together a co-ed/co-speesh team to compete in the BTU Spring Olympics. Check your dormitory bulletin board and your college announcements for team sport sign-ups.

Freshman tip:
No lifts. No lines. No problem.
BTU's downhill ski area at Mount Judgment operates via an
Aethereal Tow, a safe and well-established in-between that pulls
you up the mountain faster than you can say "this is how it ends."
Adjust your goggles. Bend your knees. Hold on to your poles. This
is the only mountain in the world that offers uphill downhill skiing.

FITNESS: THE CHAPEL AT BEAR TOWNE

Don't neglect your spiritual fitness in Bear Towne—it's the last place you want to be if your soul detaches. With so many scavengers on campus, your soul would be harvested faster than you can say, "No, Mr. Yeti, I am not a chew toy."

Location: The Bowl at the center of campus

Hours: Open 24/7

Services:
Nondenominational soul maintenance: daily
Confession: daily

Other denominational and religious services vary. Check the church bulletin for the current schedule.

WHAT TO DO IF YOUR SOUL PEELS UP

If you suspect your soul may be lifting, stop what you are doing and immediately report to the campus chapel.

BEAR TOWNE BOOKSTORE

BTU's bookstore carries more than just books and class materials. Here, you can also find basic toiletries and first aid, Bear Towne University merch, snacks, and survival gear.

Freshman tip: GO EARLY! The bookstore usually runs out of essentials during orientation week!

Location: The Trinity Center in The Bowl

Hours:
Mon-Fri 0800-1900
Sat-Sun 1000-1600

Bear Towne University's student newspaper, *The Campus Legend*, is your best source for campus news, social drama, questionable predictions, and wildly irresponsible "investigative journalism."

It's published monthly, and you can pick up a copy at Chinook Hall, the Trinity Center Bookstore, and in most dorms.

Equal parts public service and paranormal rumor mill, *The Legend* covers everything from the weather and hockey scandals to suspicious disappearances, sudden structural shifts in Olde Main, and "alleged" Aethereal anomalies. If you want to know what's happening at BTU before it happens to you, read it. If you want to preserve your sanity, take it with a grain of salt.

Founded by BTU librarian Ava Spitz in 1930, the paper is an ever-evolving archive of campus life written in ink, urgency, and rumor. It reports on lectures and avalanche alerts, disappearances and discoveries, hockey victories and hospitalizations, and the quiet catastrophes that never make it into an I-MET report. In a place like Bear Towne, truth is rarely clean and never complete, and *The Legend* does not pretend otherwise.

The Campus Legend is always on the lookout for great talent. If you're a photographer, aspiring journalist, or simply like to write about odd things, join the staff!

For more information, contact the editor-in-chief:
Mrs. Ava Spitz, BTU Librarian

VIII. CAMPUS HAZARDS AND PECULIARITIES

THE TUNNELS AT BTU: AVOID THE COLD

<u>Lighted Tunnels</u>

Alaska gets cold. Not "cute scarf weather" cold. More like negative-40-degrees-and-your-fingernails-have-snapped-off cold.

Most of the buildings at BTU are connected by a network of lighted underground tunnels, so you can travel across campus without setting foot outside.

Use the tunnels.

Because frostbite is painful, and hypothermia will kill you faster than a vacuum glazed in-between.

<u>Dark Tunnels</u>

Stay out of the dark tunnels.

THE GAZEBO

I-MET Entry 67-B: The Gazebo
Hazard Level: 0 / Mildly Annoying; Occasionally Mortifying
Location: Eastern Arboretum / Aether Grove
Established: Post-event / May 1953
Classification: Cottonwood Remnant / Aetheric Echo
Status: Stable / Contained (mostly)
Faculty Oversight: Dr. Simeon Woodfork

I-MET Report:

Unintentional result of unsanctioned use of Aethereal dust.

- Fatalities: 17
- One building destroyed / One structure created

"The student attempted to 'teach' the Aethereal Cottonwood to speak, but instead encouraged the carnivorous tree to organize his grove in a rebellion against the university. As the experiment resulted in multiple fatalities to humans, human-like non-humans, and Aethereal creatures alike, including both the student and her test subject, the student's project was marked FAILED. However, the student was posthumously conferred her degree for extraordinary effort and research, resulting in an addition to the university's list of THINGS NOT TO DO." — *Excerpt, End-of-Year Faculty Council Minutes, 1953.*

THE CHATTERING GAZEBO

ALL YOUR SECRETS LAID BARE

(Originally published in *The Bear Towne Campus Legend*, Fall 1955.)

Everyone remembers where they were on the night the forest attacked. This journalist was enjoying a delightful cup of hot Ooze with a dash of cinnamon at the Bruised Moose Café when the trees cut the power. What followed was bedlam and blood.

When the dust settled, Bear Towne University had lost 17 souls and gained one memorial to reckless research, officially named The Ethel Treadwell Memorial Gazebo, but quickly dubbed The Chattering Gazebo by the BTU class of 1954.

The night the forest attacked will no doubt swiftly fade into campus legend, and in so doing become vulnerable to exaggeration and disbelief.

As I bore witness to this tragedy and as I hold in my possession Miss Treadwell's laboratory notes and personal journals, it falls to me to set down the true story of the events that created the Chattering Gazebo in the hope that future generations remember what we learned at such a terrible cost.

The nosy object, which now sits innocuously on the southwestern edge of the northeast leaf, was not always a gazebo. Once upon a time, it was a clever, if not discontented, tree.

And Ethel Treadwell was the loneliest girl on campus.

***

Ethel Treadwell wanted nothing more than a miracle for finals and a friend she could trust. In the end, she got neither and both at once.

Like so many Aethereal deviants, Ethel had come to Bear Towne University with the great hope that she would find her place in the world, or rather her place between the human and non-human worlds, when she did not neatly fit into either.

Part human and part Púca with no control over her body hair, no skill at shape-shifting, and pestilent bad breath, Ethel found it increasingly difficult to make friends.

She did, however, have a great talent for ParaBotany and a callous disregard for campus rules. So instead of testing her approved fertilizers on Earthly trees inside the containment greenhouse as her end-of-term project, Ethel stole Professor Thumb's supply of Aethereal dust, created an unauthorized Aethereal drug, marched into the White Forest alone, and trapped a carnivorous tree.

Her goal was twofold: she would create a trustworthy companion, and she would present said companion to her ParaComm professor as her conversation partner, thereby finally earning a passing grade.

Ethel closed her mouth, and before she approached the snared tree, she waited exactly thirty-three minutes in her blind in a White Forest spruce. That was twenty minutes longer than it typically took her breath to dissipate in a no-wind environment, and the only valuable procedure she'd learned from her third attempt at passing her ParaComm class. It was now safe—for the tree at least—for Ethel to approach her test subject.

It was a yearling, an Aethereal cottonwood by looks of it, and not at all charmed to find its cursorial root ensnared in a golden trapline.

At approximately eight feet tall, it towered over Ethel, and it snarled its frustration, flailing its branches wildly.

Ethel remained well outside its reach as she prepared her Aethereal dust-infused mycelium spray. She'd worked since September on the formula, recombining critical fungal DNA with the Púca chromosomes responsible for coordinating a shape-shift, and infusing the new genetic material into a virus.

The theory was sound.

The new virus created a subconscious-level super-communication link between two entities. She'd already tested a small amount of the concoction on a bell pepper plant, which had relayed to her that it had finished producing nuts for the season. She was sixty-two percent confident in that result, and she theorized that a larger test subject would "speak" more clearly than a small pepper plant.

That the pepper plant was never capable of producing nuts in the first place hadn't seemed worth a mention in her lab notebook.

Ethel wanted to comfort the tree—to reassure it that she meant it no harm—but if she opened her mouth, her breath would damage its bark, and besides, the whole reason she'd ensnared the tree in the first place was because trees didn't understand verbal communication.

Not yet.

The tree struggled against the trapline in a tantrum, thrashing at the ground, but Ethel had used gold, which confuses carnivorous trees. It couldn't distinguish the line from the ferns it trampled, and it carried on like this for several hours.

Ethel waited just out of reach, patiently taking notes, until finally the tree let out a mournful groan, plunged its roots deep into the ground, and fell asleep.

To the untrained eye, it may have looked in that moment like an ordinary tree, basking in Alaska's springtime sun, leaves lightly clapping with the breeze.

But then there was its mouth, a bear trap embedded in its trunk.

Ethel tiptoed slowly through the brush and closer to the young cottonwood, eyes glued to its teeth and placing each step deliberately, careful not to tread over the buried roots.

She hoisted her atomizer high, aiming the nozzle at the tree's mouth, which opened and closed in a gentle cadence. At the perfect moment, when she was less than a foot away, she squeezed the actuator and let loose the fungal-virus, which shot through the air in a sticky slime stream and into the wide-open mouth of the unsuspecting tree.

The tree sputtered when the spray hit the back of its throat, but then it swallowed loudly, much like one does after accidentally inhaling an insect.

Ethel locked her lips around the atomizer, bit off the loose end of the slime stream, and drank it down, completing the Púca-to-tree communication link.

What came next is pieced together from Ethel's journals, faculty notes, the surviving fragments of the ParaBotany lab's I-MET report, the testimonies of three traumatized sophomores, and the ramblings of The Chattering Gazebo.

For a moment, nothing happened.

Ethel stood there in the pale spring sun, one hand still on the actuator, the other hovering uselessly at her side, as if she might pet the cottonwood like a dog. The trapline glinted around the tree's roots. Its branches drooped lazily. Its mouth hung open, slack and wet, as if it were fast asleep and dreaming.

Then Ethel's stomach turned. Not with nausea or fear. With *information.*

A voice entered her head—not words exactly, but a sensation like bark splitting, like sap moving, like hunger learning its own name.

ALONE.

The word came like a threat. Ethel stumbled backward, boots scuffing the moss.

The tree opened its eyes, dark knots against a pale bark that squinted and fixed on her with an intensity that stole her courage. The tree's attention slid into her, and it felt an awful lot like a constrictor encircling its prey.

She had wanted a friend, but this was all wrong.

The cottonwood flexed its branches, but the trapline held. It thrashed once, twice, and then it stilled and tilted its head as if listening.

Ethel listened back.

At first, the communication was crude: stark images of the sun and the sky, pungent scents of bear scat and rotting leaves. Then the emotions joined: the sweet memory of blood in soil, the satisfaction of crunching bone, the ache of winter starvation.

As the fungal virus threaded itself deeper into the tree's nervous system, the tree's disjointed thoughts came together. The cottonwood was learning language the way a predator learned weakness.

Another word rumbled inside Ethel's head.

HUNGRY.

Ethel's heart hammered. She should have left. She should have run back to campus, to the containment greenhouse, to Professor Thumb, to anyone with a shred of authority and a working sense of self-preservation. But Ethel Treadwell had been lonely for too long. And the tree, however impossible it seemed, was lonely too, she reasoned. What else could "hungry" mean in this context but lonely?

She swallowed. Her mouth tasted of fungus and dirt and the faint metallic tang of Aethereal dust. She forced her thoughts into something pleasant and shaped like speech.

Welcome, she tried.

The cottonwood's mouth opened wide. Its tongue, if you could call it that, shifted like a loose plank, tasting the air before it made a sound, and Ethel actually inched closer to hear it.

It wasn't a word this time, but a chatter. A rapid clicking as its teeth gnashed together again and again, which may have been mistaken for a thousand small twigs snapping in the wind.

Ethel flinched, but she steadied herself. Her breath came faster, and she remembered too late that her breath was poison to delicate bark.

The cottonwood recoiled slightly as if confused, then irritated, and the connection surged.

Ethel felt the tree's irritation bloom into something bigger. It was no longer hungry. It was now insulted. And through the link, Ethel tasted something else—something that dropped her stomach.

The cottonwood didn't think of itself as a tree. It thought of itself as a *grove*, a network, a family. It thought of the other cottonwoods deep in the White Forest as extensions of itself. Not merely sisters, brothers, and elders, but as conjoined twins with shared experiences and shared pain. It felt their roots through the Earth like hands holding hands. It felt their peace, their hunger, and…

The forest floor shifted around her. A flock of tiny birds exploded out of a nearby birch, and a mighty thump shook the ground. Ethel hadn't created a communication link between herself and one tree. She'd created a link to all of them. And they were using it. They were talking. But not to her—to each other.

The cottonwood gave her a sly leer, and Ethel understood immediately. It was rage with a tinge of glee. The tree reveled in the grove's anger at the humans who had cut them, harvested them, and even burned them when they'd grown too numerous.

The virus had done more than open a channel—it had widened one. The subconscious link did not merely share thoughts; it equalized them. Her human fears mixed with his feral instincts. His hunger mixed with her loneliness. Her yearning to be understood mixed with his yearning to obey the old, buried call of a wrathful forest.

And then Ethel made her final, fatal mistake.

Worried that the tree might slip free once it recovered its strength, she attempted to teach it a rule. A simple guiding phrase. She tried to explain that she didn't want the tree to confront anyone—not her, not the faculty, not the other students. She wanted peace. But her thoughts, muddled with his unfamiliar instincts, muddled with guilt, muddled with hope, and twisted into something else: *wrong*.

WRONGED, it echoed, but before Ethel could correct it, the cottonwood chattered again—faster. It opened its limbs and tilted its face up to the sky.

Ethel pressed her hands to her ears, but the sound was in her skull; in her teeth.

REVENGE.

Ethel backed away, trembling.

Somewhere far behind her, deep in the White Forest, another chittering joined the cottonwood. Then another. Then a third, until the whole valley filled with a faint clicking, like distant applause slowly drawing near.

Finally Ethel felt the urge to run. She lifted her leg, but her foot snapped back to the ground, entangled in a web of slithering roots.

The tree snapped its neck down, squinting at Ethel as it stared her down. It lurched against the trapline again, but this time it didn't thrash. It stepped. It lifted its roots, carefully and deliberately, as if it had finally recognized the line not as a fern or a vine, but as an obstacle. Seeing it as Ethel saw it, as something that could be navigated.

Gold confuses carnivorous trees. But Ethel realized too late that confusion was not the same as stupidity.

The cottonwood slid out of the trapline and straightened itself, letting out a mighty screech as Ethel tugged her foot against the entanglement of roots.

ATTACK. ATTACK. ATTACK.

At the same time it commanded the grove to move, the tree sent out a dark, alarming strategy, and Ethel panicked.

She needed to break the communication link. She spit; she gagged; she clawed at her mouth as if she could yank the virus out of her body—but it was no use. The virus had already taken hold.

The cottonwood put its face in hers and brought its branches close much like a boxer preparing to strike.

Ethel did the only thing she could think of. She opened her mouth and screamed, unleashing a bark-burning cloud of noxious gas that enveloped them both.

The cottonwood staggered back, and Ethel wriggled her foot free. She sprinted through the snowmelt and moss toward campus, lungs burning, the bitterness of fungus and bile rising in her throat.

The forest thundered behind her. The chattering of a thousand twigs multiplied with every step she took as more cottonwoods joined the chorus.

By the time she reached the first campus trail marker, the sound was everywhere. It was coming from behind her, from beside her, from beneath her, as if the spruce and fir were learning the language too.

Ethel stumbled into The Bowl like a half-mad prophet. Some students stared; some frowned. A few—the ones with enough ParaScience in their veins to recognize danger—backed away.

Ethel tried to warn them. She drew in a sharp nasal breath, but the moment she opened her mouth, her Púca breath curled out like a curse. The paint on the lamppost to her left peeled, but her warning was working. Most students turned and ran. Some froze in place and gagged; some flung an elbow over their faces and ducked into Trinity Square, but most were scattering.

The chattering surged.

The grove had found her, and through her, it found the campus.

She took cover behind Trinity Square, crouching against the rough brick wall as she scratched her final thoughts into her journal. It was a jumbled mix of Ethel's observations and regrets, the grove's tactics and goals, her fears and the trees' ambitions, but it remains the best explanation of what was to come, with her final entry proclaiming, "Everyone will DIE. Stop. WE WON'T STOP. Success is merging. DEATH IS ROOTING."

***

The carnage began when the lights cut out.

First it was the electric lights. The trees took down the line. Then they darkened the sky.

Witness Account:

> *You can't imagine it, and I can't tell you how it happened, but the sky went black. The blackest black. And it wasn't pollen or smoke or clouds… I think it was something Aethereal…some kind of light-sucker or anti-glow or some other thing. It was like the sun and stars disappeared. You can't imagine the screams and the darkness. It was the scariest thing I've ever seen.*

Next, the wind rose, and the trees moved in. The cottonwoods came down from the White Forest in a black tide of roots and snapping mouths. They barreled through campus smashing everything in their path: Earthly trees, light poles, even the concrete statue of the university mascot. They swung their burls like wrecking balls through the brick walls of Trinity Square, and they whipped their roots like medieval war flails.

A fire started in the chapel, which cast an eerie, flickering glow on the walkways.

The slower students fell first. One tree punched a branch through a geology student's belly and hoisted him high. He made a wet, surprised sound and then fell silent. The aluminum dome of his hard hat flashed in the firelight as it bobbled in the air, his boots kicking uselessly against nothing.

Another tree arced a branch like a bone scythe, harvesting three students in one smooth motion, while another two disappeared into the spiraled jaws of a monstrous Sitka spruce. Sap mixed with blood in sticky pools in the dirt, and by the time faculty responders arrived, The Bowl was a cacophony of death with bodies strewn across the quad and every structure either damaged, destroyed, or on fire.

I-MET pulled four injured students from the battlefield, and in the center of the chaos, Professor Thumb, wearing his gas mask and a suit of leather armor, stationed himself protectively between the cottonwood and Ethel Treadwell, who stood shaking so hard she looked like a moth pinned to velvet.

The cottonwood took a swipe at the professor just as he lifted his motorized saw, which sheared its largest root. Sap gushed like arterial spray, and the tree staggered back. Ethel, still bound through the link, grasped her leg with both hands and wailed as if she'd experienced the wound herself.

Professor Thumb didn't hesitate. He yanked the saw back, revved the motor, and stepped into the cottonwood's reach as if he'd done this a hundred times, which, given Bear Towne University's incident log, was entirely possible.

The tree lunged.

Thumb ducked and rolled under a whipping root, coming up on one knee with the saw angled like a knight's lance. He drove it into the cottonwood's trunk.

The sound that followed was not the clean snarl of a blade through wood, but more a scream. It came from Ethel.

She collapsed to the ground as if the saw had split her spine, her fingers clawing at the grass. Her mouth opened wide and her breath poured out in a pale, poisonous cloud.

Thumb jerked his mask toward the nearest responders.

"Get the students away from the grove," he barked. "Now!"

Two I-MET medics sprinted forward with goggles and respirators, leather gloves up like shields. They hooked an unconscious student under his arms and dragged him backward across the quad.

The cottonwood snapped its mouth open and shut, chattering so violently that its teeth splintered. The grove answered at once. All around campus, in the darkness, cottonwoods clicked in chorus.

Ethel's body convulsed. Her eyes rolled back, then snapped forward again, focused on nothing and everything at once. "MERGE," she groaned, and the grove surged forward in a rush of pale trunks and snapping jaws.

Thumb swore low and vicious, and then he did something that would be described in the official report as "an act of desperate containment." Survivors remember it in a more honest light: the moment the professor decided to build a gazebo out of a murder-tree.

The professor charged at the cottonwood as it reared up to strike, and as he lunged, he pulled a small canister from his belt, about the size of a thermos and marked with a red wax seal and the words, CONTAINMENT GAS — FACULTY USE ONLY.

He slammed the canister into the ground, and the seal broke with a hiss.

Aethereal sleeping gas poured out like smoke, spilling over the grass in a low, rolling wave.

The grove hesitated. Every cottonwood on campus—every carnivorous mouth, every whip-root, every snapping branch—paused mid-motion as if a single invisible hand had clenched around the forest's throat.

Ethel's body arched, her spine curved like a drawn bowstring.

Her mouth opened, and a low moan came out.

Thumb's voice cut through the darkness. "Ethel!" he shouted.

The cottonwood's eyes locked on him.

Thumb pointed the saw at its mouth like a teacher with a ruler. "You will stop!"

He looked past the cottonwood, beyond the black tide of trunks, to the edge of the arboretum where the grove had come from. He lifted his free hand, finger pointing toward the ground, and he made a motion like he was telling a dog to sit.

The dust thickened; the darkness seemed to bend, and the air turned heavy and metallic.

But the grove… obeyed.

At first, it was only the cottonwood in front of him. Its roots stilled. Its branches lowered. Its mouth closed.

Ethel's body slackened with it, as if the gas had loosened the noose around her nervous system.

Then, one by one, the other cottonwoods froze in place across campus. Some were mid-swing. Some were half-embedded in brick walls. Some still held students in their jaws.

Bodies fell, some alive. Some not.

Thumb's gas was not merely a sedative—it was a binding agent. The grove's roots sank not into the earth, but into something else. Faculty notes confirm they took hold in that layer of reality most people don't know exists: the in-between, a portion of our dimension that is so close to the veil between worlds, it has its own laws of physics.

Ethel's eyes fluttered open.

For a moment, just a moment, she looked like a human girl. A lonely, trembling student kneeling in a torn lab coat, hair wild, face streaked with dirt and sap and tears.

Thumb crouched beside her. Even through the gas mask, his voice softened. "Ethel," he said.

She blinked at him slowly, and her lips moved. A whisper came out, thin and ragged, "I… did it," she said.

Thumb's shoulders sagged. "Yes," he murmured. "You did."

And then, Ethel collapsed—the Púca mind not meant to bear the entire instinctive consciousness of a carnivorous cottonwood grove amplified by Aethereal dust.

The cottonwood shuddered, and Thumb stumbled back. Around Ethel, the tree twisted its limbs, curling downward like arms reaching to gather her in. Its trunk thickened, and its bark split as it reshaped into latticework. Branches snapped, then reformed, twisting into rafters. Roots curled up and around, in a frantic, desperate architecture, braiding themselves into spiraling supports and spreading outward,

flattening and weaving and locking into a circular base.

The grove went quiet.

Ethel groaned, "friend." It was a long, breathy exhale, and then her body went still with her eyes frozen open and her mouth slightly parted.

The grove absorbed her death like water and settled into the earth. The cottonwood died standing, so to speak, its consciousness collapsing into Aetheric residue trapped within the wood.

When the sky cleared and the light returned, the faculty found, in the center of the ruined quad, a gazebo. A perfect octagonal structure of pale wood and braided roots with a roof made of interlocked cottonwood limbs and benches carved from trunk and burl. In the heart of it, where a human architect might have placed a plaque, lay a knot of bark shaped like a mouth. A terrible, lovely thing.

The cottonwood exists only as an echo now—an Aetheric resonance bound to the wood and Púca. A remnant mind, disembodied and confused. Ethel, unable to converse and lonely to the end, became the thing that "talks," and the university turned a massacre into a quaint landmark.

In the days to come, the gazebo would whisper.

At first, the survivors assumed it was simply the settling of wood. A creak. A snap. A natural sound.

But then the muttering started.

A sophomore claimed she heard her own name—first, middle, and last—spoken through the gazebo's knotted mouth.

Faculty dismissed it as "long-resolved auditory pareidolia."

But then a professor swore it repeated, in perfect cadence, the private insult he'd mumbled about the dean at Olde Main.

A grieving mother visiting the memorial collapsed sobbing when the gazebo chattered the last words her son had said to her before he'd left for campus. And one night, when a student sat alone inside it after curfew, crying over a flunked exam and the cold, dark melancholy of winter, the gazebo leaned close, impossibly close, and clicked a single, unmistakable word into the night.

PATHETIC.

***

Seventeen died in minutes: thirteen students, one faculty member, one visiting scholar, one no-luck hare, and one carnivorous tree.

The university did what it always did. It renamed. It reclassified. It rebranded.

And then it held a memorial service and planted flowers. Officially, the structure was christened: The Ethel Treadwell Memorial Gazebo.

But students named it something more fitting: The Chattering Gazebo.

The faculty declared it stable and contained (mostly).

In the years that followed, Dr. Simeon Woodfork, who was assigned oversight of the anomaly, wrote the final note in the I-MET record: The structure appears to be an Aetheric echo of the original grove consciousness, bound in place by residual dust.

It doesn't move, but it does listen. And it remembers. The cottonwood is dead. But the bond it formed with Ethel was never severed. Ethel's death may have ended the carnage, but it started the haunting.

To the typical freshman, the gazebo looks like any carved masterpiece: impressively innocent. But be advised. The moment you step near it, the air changes. The cottonwood listens to the small, guilty corners of your mind where you keep the secrets you never tell anyone, not even yourself. And then the gazebo chatters.

Faculty may have formally classified the Chattering Gazebo as "mildly annoying," but this newspaper disagrees. Call it cursed. Call it a confessional. But know that this is the place where your soul is briefly held up to the light and judged by something that will savagely humble your pride and happily destroy your reputation.

If you look closely at the knotted mouth, you'll see a warning scrawled in small, shaky cursive, as if written by someone who still felt the harsh sting of social isolation, or perhaps the jagged prick of bark splintering behind their eyes: All your secrets laid bare.

END-OF-ENTRY FACULTY ADDENDUM

NOTE: Students are reminded that the gazebo is not a "ritual site," a "truth booth," or a "fun dare." Any student caught loitering inside the structure after dusk will be fined and assigned three hours of containment greenhouse duty.

THE HOSPITAL AT BEAR TOWNE

I-MET Entry 199: The Hospital
Hazard Level: 6
Location: ParaMedicine Leaf
Established: 1985
Classification: Aethereal Necrotizing Mutation
/ Aetheromyces necrophagus (Infectious Variant)
Status: Active
Faculty Oversight: Dr. Luna Starr

I-MET Report:

Flesh-Eating Zombitis (FEZ) is a rare but documented Aethereal-adjacent fungal infection caused by the Aetheromyces necrophagus microbe and observed in patients treated within the BTU Hospital emergency department. A highly infectious strain that spreads with alarming speed and is associated with extremely high mortality.

While conventional necrotizing infections occur in non-liminal environments, FEZ appears correlated with elevated Aethereal saturation, barrier instability, and post-traumatic energetic exposure.*

** Translation: It's not the zombie apocalypse, but it will kill you just the same.*

THE LIBRARIAN AT BEAR TOWNE

I-MET Entry 80-A: Spitz, Mrs. Ava, Librarian
Hazard Level: 0 / Staunch
Location: BTU Library / Adjacent Grounds
Established: November 1954
Classification: Partial Zombie / Outcome Negotiator
Status: Active
Faculty Oversight: None

I-MET Report:

Unintentional result of unsolved attempted murder. Assailant punctured subject's back with an Aetherinum-infused blade.

- Fatalities: 1 (partial)

"Subject presents no measurable threat to student population and has demonstrated statistically significant reductions in fatal and catastrophic incidents within BTU. Partial Zombie classification (non-contagious, stable, self-regulating) is considered administratively negligible and requires no active containment. Of greater relevance are the documented instances of outcome deferral, near misses, and incident redistribution occurring in temporal proximity to Subject." – *Excerpt, End-of-Year Faculty Council Minutes, 1965.*

MRS. SPITZ

THE CUSTODY OF CONCLUSIONS

(Originally published in *The Bear Towne Campus Legend*, Fall 1989.)

Imagine that your campus librarian knows more about you than your roommate does.

More than your friends.

More than your family.

More than you know about yourself, and you've never questioned it.

Of course she knows things. That's her job. She is surrounded by volumes of knowledge, and as editor-in-chief of the campus tabloid, she obviously hears all the gossip. Plus, she knows which books you check out, which ones you return late, which ones you file on your bookshelf and pretend you've finished, and which ones you reported as "lost" because you loved the quirky characters so much you couldn't part with the book.

She knows you prefer the third-floor carrels by the windows. She knows you skip breakfast on Tuesdays. And after that arrogant hockey player broke your heart last November, she knows you cried in the stacks and pretended it was allergies.

Mrs. Spitz has always known everything.

You tell yourself that's comforting.

But one afternoon, while waiting for her to unlock the archive room, you notice something odd. On her desk sits a thin manila folder. Your name is typed neatly on the tab with a hyphen and the word *drowned*.

Not handwritten. Typed.

You stare at it for a moment and then laugh it off. Of course she keeps records. Book records. Borrower records. Newspaper records. Perfectly normal records.

But later that week, when you hand her a book you found lying in the quad, she doesn't take it. Instead she smiles gently. "I thought you might like that ending better."

You glance down.

It's a backcountry hiker's survival story.

You look up.

Mrs. Spitz is stamping another return, nonchalant.

"I think you misunderstood," you begin, setting the book on her desk. "I found this—"

"—exactly when you should have," she says. The smile remains. "But some conclusions require editing."

Your gaze drifts to the folder still sitting on her desk.

Your name.

A hyphen.

Drowned.

The folder is somehow thinner now.

Outside, a delivery truck lurches past the front steps, brakes screaming. Someone slips on the marble staircase, but catches themself with a startled, "whoa." A ladder clatters somewhere against a bookshelf.

Normal campus sounds. Normal almosts.

Mrs. Spitz presses her palm flat on the folder and squeezes her eyes shut.

Then she reaches for her stamp and brings it down with quiet authority.

"Due," she says softly, sliding the book back to you, "is not the same as inevitable."

You don't ask for an explanation. You only notice, as you collect your book, that the hyphen on the tab is gone. As is the word after it.

And you understand that survival here has a custodian.

OLDE MAIN

I-MET Entry 10: Olde Main
Hazard Level: 3
Location: ParaScience Leaf
Established: 1797
Classification: Active In-Between / Threshold Negotiator / Weather Vane
Status: Active
Faculty Oversight: Dr. Simeon Woodfork

I-MET Report:

Original foundation survey indicates construction over documented Aethereal seam, causing a large, persistent, and active but stable in-between. Facility exhibits periodic lateral inclination during high-velocity wind events, though these yaws seem confined to the exterior of the building. Structural integrity remains uncompromised. No material fatigue detected.

- Disappearances: 4 (all recovered and accounted for)
- Injuries: 184 (mostly minor)

Containment deemed impractical.
Disruption not advised.

ODE TO OLDE MAIN
BY AVA SPITZ, 1926

I have watched Olde Main incline—
not break, not crack, not bend.
It leans as if to overhear
what rides the northern wind.

It tilts toward thresholds no one sees,
toward fractures in the sky;
its rafters groan not out of pain
but in a sure reply.

When violet splits the ridge at night
and thins the Arctic air,
the in-betweens slide through the seams
Olde Main must always share.

Twelve went in at evening bell.
None came out again.
The records say the floors held fast.
The floors say they fell in.

Count the beams—there will be twelve.
Always twelve in view.
But when it leans, a darker rib
appears between the two.

Not wood. Not light.
Not wholly there.
A shape too thin to name.
It watches from the in-between
and waits to be let in.

THE WHITE FOREST

White Forest — Travel Advised Only During Daylight

I-MET Entry 1-WF: The White Forest
Hazard Level: Varies
Location: Northwest Leaf / Aethereal Seamline Corridor
Established: Pre-Charter
Classification: Sentient Biome w/Threshold Ecology
Status: Active
Faculty Oversight: Prof. Edgar Thorne

I-MET Report:

The White Forest predates Bear Towne University and cannot be removed, relocated, or meaningfully discouraged. Because it sits within a documented Aethereal seam, new creatures, conditions, and hazards constantly appear and evolve. Weather patterns do not behave meteorologically.

- Confirmed Fatalities/Disappearances: 72*
- Injuries: 398 (minor-critical)

The forest demonstrates selective predatory response to non-native humans and auditory mimicry.

* Students from "Outside" should travel through the White Forest only when escorted by a non-human.

WHITE FOREST HAZARDS

- **Alder Hell:** Deep Aethereal undergrowth producing braided "false" trails and tripping hazards.

- **Black Bears:** Curious, strong, and occasionally maltempered. Can be Earthly or Aethereal. Never surprise or taunt a bear. Never run from a bear. Never feed or pet a bear.

- **Black-Eye-Fly:** Swift, painful bites cause irritation and temporary blindness.

- **Carnivorous Trees:** Eats only during waking hours and prefers non-Alaskan human meat. Confused by gold. Trees demonstrate measurable hesitation around certain creatures.

- **Devil's Club:** Toxic and unsafe for casual handling. All stems and leaves have sharp spines, which can pierce skin and inject irritants, causing inflammation, swelling, and infection.

- **Man-Eating Trees:** Cousin to the Carnivorous Tree and extremely rare. Hums. Prone to cooperation.

- **Mosquitoes:** Both the common Alaskan species and Aethereal mutants. Mosquitoes kill more students (eventually) than all other hazards at BTU combined. Use repellent.

- **Mad Cow Parsnip:** Contains furanocoumarins and cause phytophotodermatitis, leading to blistering, itching, skin burns, and eventual Vampyritis, if left untreated. Activated when the sap comes into contact with skin and is then exposed to sunlight.

- **Mud & Muskeg:** Deep, boot-sucking bogs trap unsuspecting hikers.

- **White Forest Yeti:** Largely reclusive. Extremely territorial. Most hibernate until winter, though some seem to enjoy warmer weather.

- **Acoustic Distortion:** Sound waves, like the weather, do not obey normal physics in the White Forest. Be aware.

- **Avalanche:** Even a small avalanche can be fatal in a gully or bowl. Always check the I-MET trail reports before embarking.

- **Cornices:** Will teach you the acceleration of gravity without warning. Don't mistake an overhanging snow shelf for solid ground.

- **Frostbite:** Better than a yeti bite but can still take a limb.

- **Hypothermia:** Causes most winter White Forest fatalities. I-MET is fast, but even they slow down in the deep snow and freezing cold.

- **Kill-Ya Cold:** -10°F to -40°F ambient temps common. Then there's the wind. Exposure results in frostbite, hypothermia, and an I-MET rescue if you're lucky.

- **Moose in a Narrow Trail:** More irritable in winter.

- **Overflow:** Water pushed up through ice and onto trails can be four feet deep.

- **Snow Drift Displacement:** Topography shifts. Trails relocate. Landmarks migrate. Lost = cold.

- **Sweat-Freeze / Lung-Freeze:** Exertion in arctic temperatures can cause ice crystals in the lungs and frozen sweat. One kills you slowly. The other's a bit quicker.

- **Tree Wells:** Deep pockets around tree trunks. Can trap and suffocate.

- **Yeti (Winter Configuration):** Hard to see. Harder to outrun. Best to steer clear. If you see breath without a body, freeze.

NOTE: The White Forest remains available to students who feel overqualified for indoor survival. Participation in outdoor misjudgment is optional. Consequences are not.

CAMPUS IN-BETWEENS

I-MET Entry 7-A,B,C: Persistent In-Betweens
Hazard Level: Varies
Locations:
- Olde Main
- Tunnel #7
- Mount Judgement ski area
Established: 1796+
Classification: Enduring Veil Rarefaction / Micro Tear
Status: Active
Faculty Oversight: Fr. Dr. Vesper Anselm

I-MET Report:

Three localized distortions of the veil separating the Earthly plane from the Aether causing temporal and/or Aethereal displacement have persisted on BTU grounds for more than a century. An asterisk on the campus map marks the location of the three active in-between zones. They are mostly harmless.

UNMARKED IN-BETWEENS

I-MET Entry 7-D: Unmarked In-Betweens
Hazard Level: 10
Location: Campus-wide (most active during break-up)
Established: 1797+
Classification: Unstable Veil Rarefaction / Micro Tear
Status: Active and Transient
Faculty Oversight: Fr. Dr. Vesper Anselm

I-MET Report:

Small, unmarked in-betweens tend to appear and disappear here and there around campus during the spring months especially, though not exclusively.

This remains a low-frequency but high-consequence phenomena with unpredictable outcomes.

NOTE: I-MET extraction can take anywhere from minutes to years.

Unmarked in-betweens present as:
- A sudden pressure differential and distortion in air density
- Sound dampening or over-amplification
- Temperature anomalies inconsistent with surroundings
- A pulling sensation not attributable to wind or gravity

Students have reported the impression of "stepping through something thin." Others describe it as "falling sideways," while another has reported feeling an embrace of tentacles.

Exposure to an in-between causes:
- Sudden displacement
- Temporary loss of orientation
- Auditory hallucinations
- Energetic depletion
- Unconventional physical, mental, emotional, energetic, and spiritual trauma

Should you encounter an unmarked in-between, perform a flail-beat or wait for I-MET and remain calm. Panic increases instability.

POLTERGEISTS

I-MET Entry 8-A: Free-Range Poltergeists
Hazard Level: 1+ (More than mildly annoying)
Location: Campus-wide
Established: 1795
Classification: Aetheric Echo / Residual Energetic Agitation
Status: Active / Nomadic
Faculty Oversight: I-MET

I-MET Report:

Unbound kinetic entities on the liminal plane manifest on campus as "sticky" residual Aetheric energy. Not a traditional haunting and not tied to a singular traumatic event or deceased individual.

Turbulent, impulsive, and volatile. Most focus on atypical hobbies. Many make it their mission to annoy nearby humans, especially freshmen.

Unintelligent and mostly unorganized but highly reactive.

As part of your immersive educational experience on our uniquely liminal campus, you may occasionally encounter minor Aetheric kinetic activity (commonly referred to as "Free-Range Poltergeists").

Free-Range Poltergeists are a natural byproduct of our vibrant ParaScience environment and reflect BTU's long-standing commitment to interdisciplinary boundary exploration.

What to Expect
- Light object displacement
- Noise
- Localized cold pockets
- Missing items
- Doors slamming / Books pursuing short-term flight

If you've attracted a poltergeist, expect it to stick around.

Your Role as a Responsible Student
- Maintain composure
- Avoid escalation
- Refrain from verbal antagonization
- Secure fragile heirlooms

If you experience mild kinetic disruption, consider it an opportunity to practice adaptive resilience.

Reporting Guidelines
It is not necessary to report a poltergeist unless:
- Significant bodily injury results
- Object displacement forms recognizable geometric patterns
- You perceive an imminent threat to life or property

"If it throws one book, ignore it. If it throws the shelf, relocate."

Common Misconceptions
Free-Range Poltergeists are NOT:
- Dead students
- Trying to send a message
- Assigned to your residence hall
- Harmless - Escalated poltergeist activity can cause bodily injury.

Faculty Note:
- Absence of activity does not indicate departure
- Poltergeists are not pets.
- Poltergeists do not have crushes, but they do have favorites.

Do NOT:
- Threaten a poltergeist
- Throw something back
- Ask it questions

A Final Word of Reassurance*
Poltergeists cause a small fraction of injuries at BTU. And, because of our healthy poltergeist population, most students complete their freshman year with:
- Enhanced patience
- Improved reflexes
- A deeper appreciation for gravity

* Remember: calm students experience less anxiety.

"What you call a poltergeist is merely current that refused its keeper."

Need some peace and quiet? Take advantage of the University's public use cabins in the White Forest.

THE CAMPUS BANSHEE

AN INTERVIEW WITH THE BANSHEE

(Originally published in *The Bear Towne Campus Legend*, Winter 1987.)
By Staff Correspondent M. Halloway

Bear Towne's own resident banshee has become something of a legend: a fable of terror to prospective students, a frightful mystery to newcomers, and, indeed, a bit of a curse to those who have been punished here.

At the same time, this enigmatic student has proven to be a brilliant researcher and has been credited with developing numerous life-saving remedies for humans and non-humans alike. This year, she was once again bestowed the prestigious Preserver of Life Award for her invention of the universal venom resistance patch (UVRP), a game-changer in the treatment of otherwise lethal bites from both Earthly and Aethereal creatures alike.

This reporter sat down with Giselle Goarhausen to discuss her great achievements and to separate the facts from the fears, and the truth from the superstitions surrounding our "Campus Banshee" in her first-ever, sometimes contentious two-hour interview.

***

Campus Legend: Miss Goarhausen, thank you for agreeing to this interview. You've declined requests like this for years. Why now?

Giselle: Because the university president directed it.

But also, people dismiss me out of fear or horror or whatever, and I don't want that anymore. When fear becomes louder than facts, people stop listening to both. So it's time to correct the record— at least the parts that can be corrected. I would like to be a more valued and less loathed member of this community. And my work has finally outpaced the rumors.

Campus Legend: You're referring to the rumors surrounding your… condition?

Giselle: I'm referring to the mythology people have built to avoid acknowledging my research. It's easier to call me a monster than to discuss enzyme inhibitors and cross-species coagulation.

Campus Legend: Yet you don't deny being the so-called "Campus Banshee."

Giselle: I don't deny what I am. I deny what people think that means.

Campus Legend: Let's talk about the science, then. The Universal Venom Resistance Patch—UVRP—has already been credited with saving dozens of lives.

Giselle: Hundreds, actually, if you include non-humans. That patch interrupts venom binding at the cellular level. It doesn't cure; it buys a patient time to get the antivenom. Time is what saves lives.

Campus Legend: What was your inspiration in coming up with this idea—that it was possible to stop venom from harming someone?

Giselle: It was during a hike in the White Forest. I came across an Aethereal opossum, which hadn't been documented in the literature, by the way. So I studied it. It became my semester project. I knew Earthly opossums had a natural resistance to venom, and I wondered how an Aethereal charge may have transformed that resistance. Turned out to be a breakthrough.

Campus Legend: Indeed it was. But this isn't your first Preserver of Life Award.

Giselle: No. And I doubt it will be my last—assuming the university continues to let me work uninterrupted.

Campus Legend: Interrupted by whom?

Giselle: Morons. Nitwits. Students who dare each other to prank me or break into my lab. Faculty who insist on treating me as if I'm a hazard. Administrators who threaten to punish me for lame offenses.

Campus Legend: Some would say those precautions are warranted.

Giselle: Then those people are idiots. They don't understand banshees—or medicine. I don't cause death—I sense it. There is a difference, and it matters.

Campus Legend: Still, you've been linked—fairly or not—to several…unfortunate incidents over the decades.

Giselle: Decades. An interesting word choice.

Campus Legend: You've been enrolled at Bear Towne University for—

Giselle: —a long time. Yes. I learn continuously. Medicine changes. Science evolves. So do I.

Campus Legend: You don't… age?

Giselle: Does it look like I could get any older?

Campus Legend: What I mean to ask is… Well, to put it bluntly… What would you say your age is, and are you capable of… well, dying?

Giselle: Everything dies. Including this interview. Including me. Including *you*.

Campus Legend: Of course. Do you feel your particular condition—when it comes to age that is—makes it difficult to form attachments?

Giselle: It makes it rude to assume I don't have them.

Campus Legend: Let's try this: The University's public records only list you as a senior student of pre-medicine, but there's no indication of the year you enrolled. How long have you been a student at Bear Towne University?

Giselle: Long enough to know your paper's trash.

Campus Legend: According to university records, you've never had a roommate or attended a school social function. Some students claim you curse those who cross you. Is that accurate?

Giselle: I've never cursed anyone. I'm not a witch, and consequences are not curses. If you ignore lab safety, something will eventually splash in your face. If you poke a bear, it will eventually maul you. That isn't magic—it's probability.

Campus Legend: Do you see yourself as a bear? You don't have to answer that. But there's another—shall we say—rumor on campus, one that's persisted for years and was actually referenced in an article from The Legend published in 1961. Many students believe if they even look at you, they'll die a premature death. What would you say to students who are afraid to look at you?

Giselle: You mean the article that called me a hag and pinned three student deaths on me?

Campus Legend: Actually, the title was—

Giselle: —I wouldn't waste one word on a superstitious fool masquerading as a student of science.

Campus Legend: You're remarkably calm, given the tone of some of these accusations.

Giselle: I've had a great deal of practice.

Campus Legend: Would you like to address those student deaths in 1961?

Giselle: We all make mistakes.

Campus Legend: What do you want today's students to understand about you?

Giselle: That fear is a poor substitute for curiosity. And that if they ever were to hear a banshee cry, it's not a threat—it's a warning and a blessing. One I hope they would never need.

Campus Legend: Can you tell us what it's like to be a banshee?

Giselle: No.

Campus Legend: Do you possess any strengths or powers or extra-perceptual knowledge that humans do not?

Giselle: Yes. I know when to stop asking questions.

Campus Legend: Final question. Why stay at Bear Towne University?

Giselle: Assuming I had a choice in the matter, I wouldn't stay another second. But even if I weren't on Envoy probation, I'd rather be here than on the run from scavengers.

For some of us, this campus is our only sanctuary. It's our last chance at redemption. I've felt my soul shudder and peel up, and I wake up every day wondering if it's still attached, or if it's left me completely. And this place… The students here may be annoying jackasses and nonsensical halfwits, but this campus is the only thing standing between me and Hell.

I'm going to stay here until I'm well. I'm staying until I graduate.

Campus Legend: Miss Goarhausen—Giselle—I'd love to follow up on that, but that was our final question. I hope you'll consider sitting down with me again. Thank you for your time.

Giselle: I'll see you at your funeral. And for the record? This was not my idea, and it was not fun. I only did this because I had to, and I hope you appreciate it, because I'm never doing it again. They said this article would make fewer monsters and more scientists—which is adorable, given our track record.

THE LEGION OF EARTH DWELLERS

Are you stuck on Earth? You're not alone!

The Legion of Earth Dwellers is a registered student organization for members of the Bear Towne University community who have, for one reason or another, declined to complete the traditional process of dying, departing, dissolving, ascending (or descending), or otherwise vacating the premises.

This club serves individuals who have ignored repeated cosmic suggestions to move on, and provides camaraderie and mutual support for those who remain attached to Earth long past their expiration date.

Use your "extra time" constructively! The group emphasizes problem-solving, guidance, and harm reduction for campus residents and the world at large.

After all, what fun is persistence without purpose?

Humans and non-humans welcome.

For more info, contact the club's president, Pádraig O'Shea.

ENVOYS AND THE AETHER

THE ENVOYS

You'll hear about them, and you'll pretend they're human. Everyone does until they don't.

WHAT IS AN ENVOY

An Envoy is an Earth-bound custodian of life energy and the keeper of energetic equilibrium between worlds.

They are not angels. They are not demons. They are not deities.

They are administrators of balance, and they're all business.

WHAT IS THE AETHER

The Aether is a realm of pure energy separate from Earth. It is a state of perfect equilibrium from which all life energy draws and to which all life energy returns.

It is neither moral nor emotional. Like the Heavens, it is not negotiable.

When a living entity dies, its energy transitions into the Aether. An Envoy ferries that energy out of a dying life, across the Aether, and into a forming life.

KEEP OUT!

THE SEVEN EARTH-BOUND ENVOYS

BTU is proud to call one of the Seven Envoys our founder and president. Asher the Benevolent established this university to better understand the phenomenon that brought him across the veil and onto Earth.

Nobody knows how many Envoys exist on Earth, but seven have made contact with humans.

Envoys are ancient, proud, unforgiving, powerful, God-fearing, and above all, balanced.

They value loyalty, and they do not tolerate evil.

The Seven Envoys are:
1. Asher the Benevolent
2. Theon the Loyal
3. Cobon the Clever
4. Kiya the Serene
5. Adalwolf the Veracious (renamed in later texts)
6. Isolde the Broken
7. The name of the Seventh Envoy has been lost to history.

Stone relief of the Seven Envoys, circa 800 AD

IX. LOCAL LEGENDS

Read Before You Wander

Look, you enrolled in a ParaScience university — you should expect some strange things.

This is not a liberal arts college with a ghost tour for fundraising. This is Bear Towne University. Our buildings lean. Our forest attacks. The snow occasionally rearranges itself, and if you wanted normal, you would have gone somewhere with a football team and access to an opera house.

Every school has its paranormal stories. Ours just happen to be backed by science.

We included these legends in our handbook not because we enjoy scaring freshmen (though that is a modest perk), but because legends at BTU tend to originate from hard lessons learned by people who confidently wondered, *"What's the worst that could happen?"*

The worst happened.

BTU is strange, so read these legends carefully. Laugh where appropriate, and roll your eyes if you must. But remember… you can do anything once.

THE FRIENDLY YETI

Anonymous short story based on a popular BTU legend,
published in *The Bear Towne Campus Legend*, May 1987.

There are rules for the White Forest. Some are written in the
student handbook, but most are whispered over a campfire.

For example, everyone knows you do not run from a yeti. You
shouldn't feed one, either. But there's another rule most often
forgotten, and it is this: never befriend a yeti.

And here's why.

I.

The first time Jodie Livingston saw the yeti, she froze. She
didn't scream; she didn't run. And she'd forgotten all about her
Indispensable™ Yeti Spray clipped to her belt.

With her heart pounding in her throat, she stood, mouth agape,
and stiffened into a pose much like a gunfighter in the Old West—
feet spread, elbows out, fingers splayed, eyes wide.

The yeti, who had been busy eating from a low blueberry bush,
stopped mid-chew and stared at her.

They stood on opposite sides of a fallen spruce, snow
suspended in a wind-swept drift between them. The White Forest
went quiet—not the natural quiet of a fresh snowfall, but the
listening quiet that settles near a catastrophe.

Jodie was a third-year ParaMedicine major focusing on
psychology, which meant she believed most creatures could be
understood if studied long enough.

The yeti tilted its head, and Jodie gasped.

"Hello," she breathed.

The yeti lifted one massive paw. Not quite a wave, but not a strike either, and Jodie felt a thrill jab her stomach.

Then the yeti turned and lumbered away.

II.

Jodie watched with a buzz that should have been relief. But instead of thanking God for her good fortune, she couldn't wait to see the yeti again.

It wasn't the kind of thought that arrived politely, like a reasonable plan. It came like a spark in dry brush: sudden, bright, and immediately hungry for more.

Back on campus, her hands wouldn't stop moving. She peeled off her gloves, then put them back on. She made hot tea, forgot it existed, made another, and drank it like a shot. She grabbed a fresh notebook from her shelf and scribbled her notes on the yeti encounter over four pages. Then she tucked the book under her mattress.

She told herself it was academic, a sort of clinical curiosity. She told herself she had spent enough hours listening to faculty warnings about "anthropomorphizing" the hazards at Bear Towne University. Though she knew better than to attach a human motive to an Aethereal predator, as she replayed the lifted paw in her mind, she realized it was very much like a wave. And if not a wave then at least an acknowledgment. Something almost… courteous.

And so in her notes, she reclassified this particular yeti as an "Aethereal anomaly."

Her roommate, Audrey, watched her pace in the tight floor space of their room, eyebrows climbing higher with each lap. "What happened?" Audrey asked, her voice flat, the way you ask when you already know the answer will be stupid.

Jodie stopped short and grinned, her hands balled into tight fists under her chin. "You're not going to believe this."

"Bet I will," Audrey said, one eyebrow arched.

"I saw a yeti."

Audrey blinked. "Okay."

Jodie's smile faltered. "That's it? 'Okay'?"

"People see yetis all the time."

"This one," Jodie said, stepping closer, "was different."

Audrey's face did something subtle: a slight, almost imperceptible draw in her eyebrows. Not in disbelief—she believed plenty. It was more like the expression you make when someone tells you they want to give their abusive boyfriend another chance.

"Different how?" Audrey asked.

Jodie dashed to their open door and closed it. She took Audrey's hands in hers, looked her dead in the eyes and, in a hushed voice, said, "It waved."

Audrey pulled her chin back.

Jodie nodded urgently, dropping Audrey's hands. "I said, 'hello,' and it—" She mimed the motion, lifting her hand slowly, palm out. "Like that."

"That's not a wave," Audrey said at once. "That's a paw."

"It wasn't threatening," Jodie insisted. "It didn't huff. It didn't charge. It didn't snarl. It didn't do any of those things!"

Audrey's gaze slid to the safety bulletin pinned above their desk: WHITE FOREST HAZARD ALERT: INCREASED ACTIVITY. The little doodle of a yeti in the margin looked charming in its pen-and-ink simplicity. It kind of made the danger feel manageable, like it could be boxed and captioned.

"Just because it didn't do any of those things," Audrey said carefully, "that doesn't mean it was being friendly."

Jodie scoffed. "You're always like this."

"Alive, you mean?"

"Cautious." Jodie corrected.

Audrey leaned back against her bed frame. "Jo, yetis don't do 'friendly.' They do 'hungry.'"

Jodie rolled her eyes, but her cheeks heated with excitement. "That's literally the kind of bias they teach us about. We categorize everything as dangerous because it's easier than admitting we don't understand it."

Audrey hummed. "Nooooo… We categorize them as dangerous because they eat people."

Jodie opened her mouth, then shut it, shaking her head.

Then, because she was Jodie Livingston, bright and stubborn and open-minded and somewhat morally superior to her peers, she said, "Not all of them."

Audrey stared at her.

Jodie brightened again, trying a new angle. "This could be huge. Do you know how many papers I could write? Field notes, behavioral logs… Maybe even get credit toward my master's," she said, her eyes settling in a stare into the near distance. She nodded then shook her head. "I just feel like they've been unfairly maligned, and I feel like I've just seen proof that they're not the savages the university says they are."

Audrey made a sound in her throat, which might have been a laugh if it didn't bear a note of despair. "You want to prove yetis have what… higher reasoning? Feelings?"

"No." Jodie huffed. "I just want to prove they're not mindless monsters," she said. "I want to prove the White Forest is more complex than 'don't go there alone.'"

Audrey's eyes narrowed. "So you want to go back."

Jodie raised her eyebrows, leaning in to Audrey. Then she nodded, biting her lip and squinting her eyes.

"What, you want me to go with you? — Absolutely not!"

Jodie stepped closer. "Audrey—"

"No," Audrey repeated. "I'm not going into the White Forest so you can have a personal breakthrough with a carnivorous myth."

"It's not a myth," Jodie said, shaking her head.

"That makes it worse."

Jodie exhaled. She really needed a friend to observe this breakthrough with her, but Audrey was digging in. There was only one thing left to do.

"It didn't hurt me," she said gently. It was the tone she'd learned in Psych 344 that fall. The one she used when coaxing a frightened patient into acknowledging a hard truth. "And it could have."

Audrey stared at her like she was watching someone gently pet a mouse trap. Then she rolled her eyes. "That's not—" she began, but then she stopped and clenched her jaw. "Jodie," she sighed. "That's like saying a starving lion is safe because it didn't eat you the first time you tiptoed past it. Maybe it was sick; maybe it was distracted; maybe it was—"

Jodie lifted her hands. "I'm not being reckless. I'd do it properly." She counted the ways, raising a finger for each. "During the daytime, on the trail, with a non-human friend, and I'd bring my yeti spray just in case. We'd keep our distance. I just want to see if it comes back."

Audrey shook her head. "You want to see if *you* come back."

Jodie's gaze flicked away, and Audrey saw it.

"Oh no," Audrey murmured, bringing a hand to her head. "Oh no. You're already set on this, aren't you?"

Jodie's smile returned and her eyes went wide. "I want you to come with me."

Audrey let out a slow breath. "Why?"

"Because," Jodie said, as if this were obvious, "you're my roommate. And you're practical. And you have better survival instincts. And you know the protocols." She chewed her lip a little. "And you're not human—it's perfect!"

"You want a witness," Audrey said. "A witness to your murder."

Jodie's eyes shone. "I want backup, like safety backup."

Audrey laughed once, a sharp little sound. "Safety. From your new best friend, the yeti."

Jodie plowed forward. "We'll go for twenty minutes. We'll stay near the trail. If we see it again, we leave. Simple."

Audrey's expression didn't change.

Jodie tried again, softer. "It waved, Audrey."

Audrey's gaze held hers, unblinking. "Jodie," she said quietly, "predators don't always bare their teeth to dumb students."

Jodie's grin faded. Audrey would know, being a so-called human-looking non-human predator herself. But that's why she needed her.

"Look, I'm not asking you to believe it's safe—I know it sounds dangerous," she said. "I'm asking you to make sure I don't do anything… you know… stupid while I'm out there."

Audrey stared at her, and Jodie could see her wheels turning. That was the trick. Jodie didn't need to convince Audrey the yeti was friendly. She only needed to convince her that she was going. With or without her roommate. Audrey would assume that if Jodie went alone, something horrible would surely happen. Something permanent. Audrey would care about that. She depended on Jodie during the full moon.

Audrey closed her eyes for a long moment.

Then she said, "Fine."

Jodie's face lit up.

Audrey held up a finger. "On one condition."

Jodie nodded quickly. "Anything."

"Daylight," she said. "Full gear. Spray. Flashlight. Lighter. Rope. Emergency whistle."

Jodie nodded. "That's more than one, but okay."

"No leaving the marked trail," Audrey continued.

Jodie hesitated. "But what if it's—"

"No."

Jodie nodded again.

"And if I see teeth," Audrey said, voice flat, "we leave."

Jodie rolled her eyes. "Okay, fine."

"And if it waves," Audrey added, "we still leave."

Jodie blinked. "What?"

Audrey's expression hardened. "Waving doesn't mean hello, Jodie. It could mean… anything."

Jodie laughed. "Okay, okay. We'll leave."

Audrey watched her closely. And just as Jodie was thinking that agreement was not the same as obedience, Audrey said, "Tomorrow."

Jodie clapped her hands together and smiled. "Tomorrow."

Outside, the cold wind pressed softly against the window. The glass made a faint, thin sound, like a nail tapping, testing.

III.

If their first mistake was baiting a yeti, their second was keeping it secret.

They packed quietly the next morning, moving through the dorm room like conspirators.

Jodie brought a notebook, a pen, and a bag of beef jerky. Audrey brought a lasso, two flares, and an emergency radio the size of a backpack.

Jodie clipped her Indispensable™ Yeti Spray to her belt with an exaggerated flourish, as if this were a talisman rather than a tool.

"See?" she said brightly. "Prepared."

Audrey didn't respond. She was checking batteries.

As they left the dorm, the hallway lights flickered twice, as if the building itself disapproved.

They crossed campus under a flat winter sky, boots crunching over packed spring snow. Students moved around them—laughing, hurrying.

Jodie was cheerfully talking too much, and Audrey spoke only when necessary.

At the White Forest Gate, they paused.

The entrance pillars were old wood carved with warning symbols half worn smooth, as if polished by hundreds of hands that had touched them for luck. The sign posted beside it had a recent update. Someone had added a small magic marker drawing of a beheaded hiker beneath the warning, which Audrey read aloud.

"TRAVEL ONLY DURING DAYLIGHT," she said. "DO NOT LEAVE MARKED TRAILS. DO NOT ENGAGE WILDLIFE." Audrey dipped her chin and turned a cold stare to Jodie.

"We're not engaging," she said over her shoulder, "we're observing."

Audrey tromped behind her.

As they passed under the arch, the White Forest swallowed the university bustle in what could only be described as a phenomenon. The sound of campus muted. It wasn't the gradual fade-out of distance one would expect, but an instant silence, like plunging under water.

The wet snow squished quietly under their feet, and the trees crowded close enough to make the sky feel narrow. The forest smelled of pine sap and mud this time of year, but there was the faintest hint of musk in the air.

Jodie breathed it in, eyes shining. "Do you smell that?"

Audrey did. She wished she didn't.

"It's just—" Jodie searched for a word. "Strength."

Audrey's mouth tightened. "It's a warning."

Pale pink ribbons marked the trail as it curved gently through the trees. A branch snapped to the right, and the forest on either side stilled. The birds hushed; the squirrels froze; and the small scrabbling noises in the underbrush stopped, until all that was left was just their breath and the soft *whish* of the wind.

Jodie slowed as they approached the place she'd first seen the yeti. The fallen spruce lay across the forest floor like a toppled mast, snow dusting it like powdered sugar. She stopped and pointed. "Right there."

Audrey didn't stop.

Jodie hurried to catch up. "Wait—Audrey—just look."

Audrey turned slowly, scanning the trees. "I'm looking."

Jodie stepped forward, closer to the fallen spruce. "It was right on the other side. It looked at me like—"

Audrey's hand shot out and grabbed her coat sleeve. "Don't."

Jodie looked back, her brow creased. "What?"

Audrey nodded toward the snow, and Jodie followed her gaze. Tracks.

They weren't fresh—wind had softened their edges—but they were unmistakable: large, long footprints, deep and wide, with five toes and long claws, moving parallel to the trail.

Audrey's voice came out low. "It's been patrolling."

Jodie's mouth opened wide, and she turned to Audrey. "See? It came back." She smiled triumphantly. "It was looking for me."

Audrey tracked the footprints, which never crossed the trail and her jaw flexed. "Yeah," she said. "It's probably hungry."

Jodie stepped over the edge of the trail, and Audrey grabbed her sleeve again.

"I'm just—"

Audrey jerked her back onto the path, speaking through clenched teeth. "I promised to come, and I came," Audrey said. "Now let's go."

Jodie pulled gently against Audrey's grip. "If you keep treating it like a monster, it will act like one."

Audrey stared at her. "It IS one."

Jodie's face hardened, her eyes fixed on something off the trail. And then she did something simple and catastrophic: she lifted her hand.

With her palm out and fingers curled, she waved.

For a moment, nothing happened.

The forest held its breath.

Then the trees shifted, and a pale shape stepped into view from behind a very large birch.

It seemed bigger than Jodie remembered. Its dirty fur blended into the splotchy snow, but its eyes were dark and reflective like a wet stone.

It stopped at the edge of the trail, exactly where the prints had stopped, and it looked at Jodie.

Jodie smiled, radiant.

"It came," she whispered without breaking eye contact.

"Stop staring at it, Jo—that could provoke it."

The yeti lifted its paw. Not quite a wave, but not quite something else.

"Hi," Jodie breathed.

Audrey yanked her sleeve. "And, we're leaving."

Jodie shrugged her off, still holding eye contact with the yeti. "It's not attacking," she whispered.

The yeti stepped closer. Its paw lowered slightly, palm angled toward Jodie.

"What in the name of God?" Audrey muttered.

"He trusts me," Jodie said as she stepped off the trail.

Audrey yanked her back. "No."

Jodie whirled around and wriggled her arm, but Audrey held her tight. Jodie stamped her foot. "Stop!"

"You stop. We came. We saw it. Now we go." Audrey's eyes flared.

"Audrey. It waved back—it trusts me," Jodie pleaded.

Audrey spoke low and calm. "Jodie. It hasn't attacked you, because it hasn't felt the opportunity."

Jodie's face fell.

The yeti's head tilted again, as if it were patiently listening and waiting.

Jodie swallowed. She looked back at it, then at Audrey, caught between them.

"This could change everything," Jodie said softly.

Audrey's laugh came out shaky. "Yeah. It could."

Jodie turned back to the yeti.

It lifted its paw again in the same slow motion almost-wave.

Jodie's breath hitched. "I just want to—" she whispered, peeling Audrey's fingers from her shirt. "I just want to see if it will come closer."

Jodie pulled free, and Audrey shook her head, desperate, as Jodie stepped off the trail.

The snow there was untouched, like blank paper. Her boot sank half an inch with each slow, careful step.

The yeti remained still.

Audrey stood like a statue in the trail, her fingers twitching toward the whistle in her pocket.

The yeti lowered its paw as Jodie came within reach, smiling.

"It's okay," she murmured, holding her hands out flat and turning them over. "See? It's okay."

Audrey finally moved. Her boots crunched the snow as she joined her roommate.

"Audrey," Jodie said, turning back with a triumphant gleam in her eyes and a little laugh. "It's fine."

The yeti stepped back and dipped its head before moving deeper between the trees.

Jodie's face lit up. "It wants us to follow. Audrey," she called over her shoulder, her voice bright. "Come on."

Audrey stood in the snow, heart pounding. She could've turned back. She could've run or called for help. But the forest was so quiet, and Jodie's silhouette was already slipping between trunks. Audrey knew, with sick certainty, that if she left Jodie, she would never see her again.

That's when she made the third mistake of the day.

IV.

If the trees could talk, they'd tell you the marked trail vanishes the moment you step off it.

As the girls followed the yeti around the trees and into the wilds of the White Forest, they were already lost to the world.

Jodie walked as if she were entering a sacred place—quiet, reverent, eager.

Audrey walked as if she were entering a trap—tense, hesitant, and listening for the click.

The forest changed the deeper they went. The air seemed thinner, and the snow underfoot felt less like snow and more like a deep, cold carpet. An awful stillness settled over the trio as they entered a clearing.

It was a wide, circular field of untouched white surrounded by trees like a ring of witnesses. The sky above, overcast and gray, threatened to snow. In the center of the clearing lay a shallow depression, wide and smooth, as if something heavy had rested there.

The yeti stepped to the edge of it and stopped.

Jodie approached slowly, eyes shining.

"It brought us here," she murmured in awe. "This is… its place. Where it beds down."

Audrey's gaze snapped to the snow.

The depression wasn't random; it was shaped. A deliberate nest-like bowl. A place that had been prepared.

Jodie stepped closer, and Audrey lunged after her. "Jodie—stop."

But she was already in the nest. "It trusts us," she breathed.

The yeti lowered its head, its eyes never leaving them even as a rustling in the forest grew louder behind it.

Jodie turned to Audrey, laughing softly, her face flushed with victory. "See? I told you."

Audrey didn't answer. She looked at their footprints leading into the clearing. They were already covered under a light cloud of flurries swirling down. Their path back was vanishing.

"We have to go," she said with a slow shake of her head, "or else we'll never leave, Jodie." Audrey's stare was blank and her voice vacant.

But then the yeti moved, and both girls startled.

From behind a small spruce stepped a smaller yeti, about four feet tall and wearing the face of a baby.

The larger yeti took the hand of the smaller one and led it forward, toward the girls.

Jodie's smile faded. "Audrey," she whispered, and for the first time, there was real fear in her voice.

Audrey's hands rose, instinctively—palms out, as if she could reason with teeth and hunger.

The larger yeti's nostrils flared once, slow and deliberate, and it let out a puff. The smaller one mirrored it, tiny chest rising and falling in shallow, curious breaths.

Jodie swallowed hard. "It has a baby," she whispered.

Audrey reached for the spray at Jodie's belt, but Jodie pulled away.

"Don't," Jodie breathed. "You'll scare them."

The smaller yeti dropped to all fours and stepped forward, head cocked, black eyes bright, and the larger yeti shifted its weight.

What Jodie failed to understand in that moment, what she would understand too late, is that predators do not introduce their young to friends.

They introduce them to food.

The larger yeti made a sound then—not a roar, not a snarl, but a low, guttural call that vibrated in the hollow of the clearing. The smaller one answered with a higher echo.

Not aggression… it was instruction.

Audrey moved first.

Her hand closed around the yeti spray, and she ripped it free, but Jodie grabbed her wrist. "No!"

That single second, morally sound, but catastrophically stubborn, was all the invitation her furry friends required.

The larger yeti lunged.

Snow exploded upward, and the clearing fractured into motion: white and fur and a flash of red. The girls turned to run, but there was nowhere to go that wasn't inside the nest.

Audrey's whistle shrieked once before it cut off.

Jodie's scream was shorter.

V.

Jodie Livingston did not return from the White Forest that night, and neither did her roommate.

I-MET recovered what was left of them: a severed head, a femur picked clean, and a coat, tattered and soaked in blood.

The snow in the clearing was a rough field of white tinged pink with no sign of a struggle.

Two pairs of tracks led away.

THE BLACK ROCK

A BANSHEE FAIRY TALE
(as recorded by Ava Spitz, BTU Archives, 1927)

Come closer, draw your shawl about your shoulders, and close the shutters tight, for this is no tale for bright rooms nor easy hearts…

Once upon a time, long before the banshees ever walked this world, there was an Envoy who could not bear his exile.

His name was Cobon, and he, along with many of his kind, had fallen from a realm of living light and gentle warmth into this cold world of hunger and death.

Several of the Envoys walked among mortals with careful steps. They tended what was given to them. They watched, and they waited, quite sure that they would, after a time, find their way back to the home they so deeply missed.

But Cobon did not wait well.

"We do not belong here," he would say to his brothers and sisters. "We cannot stay here. We must go home."

Longing, you see, is a blade. Held properly, it carves beauty from wood, sickness from flesh. But held too tightly, it destroys all it touches and even cuts the hand that grips it. And so begins the tale of the Black Rock.

To carve a path through the great barrier that separated the Envoys from their home, Cobon fashioned a stone of power. He gathered onyx dark as the space between the stars and quartz as pure as winter's ice, and he shaped them into a vessel smooth as bone and cold as the grave. Within it, he sealed a fleck of Aethereal gem, a spark from the Aether—the place he had lost.

But a spark alone cannot tear a hole in the world.

So Cobon did a clever and terrible thing.

He chose a mortal family whose life-power sang in a key that trembled in time with the veil between the worlds. Into the stone's hidden heart, he wove their lifelines. As with the banshees, a mortal family's life-power is passed through its women, and so, when one of the women drew their first breath of life on Earth, a thread of that life-power slipped into the rock. When one of them exhaled their last, the warmth of that ending flowed not into the Aether, but into the rock.

Generation after generation, the Black Rock drank.

It did not glow. It did not whisper. It simply waited, growing powerful with the gathered endings of a single line.

Cobon guarded that family as fiercely as any mother guards her brood. To ensure the rock would saturate in their perfect strength, he made certain the family line did not break. He bent illness aside. He thinned misfortune. He lengthened days that were meant to wane.

Indeed, even cleverness can be cruel when it refuses to let the natural song be sung.

For every portion of life he collected, the balance shifted. The Aether missed its due and murmured to him across the veil. At first it was a sweet request. Then it was a reminder. Then it was a threat.

His fellow Envoys warned him.

Among them was Kiya the Serene, whose stillness was deeper than any lake. "Abandon this," she said. "For if you pull too hard upon the veil, you will unravel both worlds."

Cobon only smiled in response—the tight smile of one who believes himself superior.

At last, the bound family bore a daughter whose life-power would fill and awaken the Black Rock. When she first touched the stone, it answered her. The centuries of gathered lifelines hummed within it like a hive in full swarm.

The stone would be full—Cobon felt it—the rock would be ripe.

One final death and the reservoir would release. The last breath of the last child would flood the vessel and split the veil like an axe through a man's skull.

And there, beyond the tear, waited his home.

But the child was young, strong, and healthy.

Cobon grew impatient.

The girl was innocent in every sense. And Cobon, who feared God even more than he missed his home, found that he could not close his hands around her tiny throat.

So he turned to one who could.

Adalwolf the Veracious had long since abandoned faith and law and mercy. He had become Adalwolf the Voracious, as his hunger for suffering was simple, and his appetite without end.

What bargain passed between them, no record keeps. Some say Cobon needed only ask Adalwolf to take the life of the child. Others say Adalwolf demanded an oath of loyalty from Cobon.

Whatever their contract, the two agreed on the night appointed to open the doorway to their home, and that's precisely how Cobon would describe it. That night, the moon was new and the sky overcast. No shadow betrayed their silent coming, and into the chamber where the girl slept, they crept.

Cobon entered first.

The wolf followed.

Cobon, unable to bring himself to witness what was to be done to the girl, whose family he'd for centuries protected from harm, stepped outside the chamber door, and turned away as Adalwolf went in.   Cobon listened as the wolf's footsteps faded into the darkness of the chamber.

For a long moment there was only silence.

Then the child stirred.

A small voice, half-asleep, asked a question no one answered.

Cobon closed his eyes and pressed his hand to the door frame. He told himself it would be quick. That it was necessary. That centuries of waiting had led to this moment, and that the veil would soon tear open.

It was little comfort.

Inside the room, Adalwolf's voice rumbled low with cruel amusement.

A bed creaked.

The younger sister whimpered.

Then came the sound of breath squeezing through a throat, the sound of a child too small to fight.

Cobon flinched, losing his resolve and fleeing the house altogether.

And then—the world split.

A crack like thunder burst from the room, followed by a light so violent it bled through windows and through the seams of the house's outer door.

Cobon staggered back.

The Black Rock screamed.

Adalwolf laughed as the child stilled.

Inside the stone, the speck of Aethereal gem—no larger than a grain of salt—awoke at last. It drank the centuries of life bound within it and reached hungrily for the moment it had been promised.

But the Black Rock was older than the wolf's hunger and more clever than Cobon's design, and in the moment the final wisp of life stretched forth from the child, the stone chose a different path.

It snapped shut, rejecting the child's life-power, and it burst in a flash of white so bright that, for the briefest moment, it erased every shadow from the world.

Adalwolf cried out.

And then he exploded.

He vanished into light and ash and bone-dust that dissipated into the night like a puff of breath on a cold day.

The Black Rock vibrated briefly as the light collapsed inward again, and then it went still.

The house was burning, and Cobon staggered back.

The veil had not opened.

But something had answered.

Far beyond the sky, in the place where the Aether presses against the skin of this world, a greater resonance stirred.

For the speck of Aethereal gem inside the Black Rock was not alone.

There are whispers, old whispers that pass between the Envoys and the ghosts that overhear their councils, that somewhere beneath the frozen lands of this earth lies a far larger Aethereal gem.

Not a shard or a fleck, but a great stone. One mighty enough to tear the veil open without the life-breath of a single mortal.

The Black Rock was but a tease.

The girl's house burned that night, and many who had come to watch the veil open fled into the darkness when Adalwolf died.

Cobon remained, though, watching through the flames, staring at the girl, the stone clutched in her hand against her chest.

His cunning had failed him.

The Black Rock had betrayed him.

The wolf had been devoured.

The way home remained shut.

But the Black Rock had tested the barrier, and somewhere hidden in the north, a greater gem waits—one that will at last send the Envoys, who do not belong on this Earth, back to their home in the Aether, and to the end of their exile.

So you'd do well to remember this: we are bound to our endings.

Cobon tried to gather endings and hoard them, to bend them toward his own desire, and in doing so, he upset the balance he so desperately longed for, and he tangled himself in a grief that has no clean release.

He walks still at the edges of forests and at the threshold of dreams. Some say he still guards the bloodline he bound. Others say he stalks the stone with a hunger sharpened by regret.

When asked of the Black Rock, mothers tell their daughters, "It is only a fairy tale," but it is not a story meant to soothe—only to warn.

Longing can open doors, but not all doors lead home. And when we tamper with endings, endings have a way of answering in kind.

X. THE INDISPENSABLE™ BRAND

If you've been at Bear Towne University for longer than five minutes, you have already encountered an Indispensable™ product.

You may not have noticed, and that's by design!

From the Luftzeug Buzzdoodles to the Out-Betweens installed in Olde Main and that Ever-Bright flashlight in your desk drawer, Indispensable™ devices are woven quietly into the fabric of campus life at BTU.

Students often ask, "Are they really indispensable?"

Statistically speaking, yes.

Indispensable™ is there for you!

Engineered for the threshold. Designed for the unexpected. And guaranteed to function in ordinary and extraordinary circumstances!

Indispensable™ specializes in Aethereal-adjacent tools, field gear, medical treatments, optical enhancement devices, and general survival equipment appropriate for our liminal campus.

All products are:

• Field-tested in Arctic conditions

• Calibrated for Aethereal drift

• Idiot-proof (to a point)

• Backed by BTU research and I-MET Operational Testing & Evaluation

Indispensable™ equipment is widely used by faculty, I-MET personnel, White Forest researchers, and students who prefer to remain corporeal.

OUR MOST POPULAR PRODUCTS*

♦ **Buzzdoodles Noise-Cancelling Earbuds: Hear What's Important**

- Calibrated especially for Luftzeug and Traumzeug travel
- Dampens annoying Earthly noise
- Allows sub-audible Aethereal bleed-through

Plug in, power up, and decide what deserves your attention!

♦ **The Ever-Bright Flashlight: Light That "Turns" the Dark**

Plug in, power up, and decide what deserves your attention!

- Multi-band light penetration
- Flicker-resistant under Aethereal compression
- Drop-tested in dark tunnels

Pairs perfectly with: The Never-Fail Lighter

Student Discount Available with Valid ID

◆ **Indispensable™ Out-Between: Campus Installed /
Faculty Approved**

Engineered for seamless exit redirection in unstable architectural
zones.

- Self-stabilizing veil alignment
- Emergency lateral ejection mode
- Minimal existential residue

Trusted in Olde Main since 1962.

◆ **Magnoggles: See What Matters**

- Enhanced Aethereal-spectrum clarity
- Northern Lights compatible
- Reduces optical distortion in seam-thin air

Is it all in your head, or is it written in the stars? Find out if your
most ardent hope is also your destiny!

◆ **Mend-a-Wound: Topical Stabilization Formula**

- Accelerates tissue recovery
- Minimizes scarring
- Retards microbial growth (including Aetheromyces necrophagus
aka flesh-eating zombitis)

Now with a pleasant odor!

♦ The Never-Fail Lighter: When It Must Work

The power of the sun on top of your head!

- Windproof
- Seamproof
- Student-proof (mostly)

Trust that when this fails, you'll already be dead!

♦ Tree Repellent: Because Not All Flora Is Friendly*

- Repels carnivorous and semi-sentient growth
- Safe for boots, backpacks, and pride
- Made of yeti urine, because trees don't like to be peed on either!

We're not sure *how* it works, but we are sure *that* it works.

(*Not effective against splinters.)

♦ Yeti Spray: Respectfully Assertive

- Non-lethal deterrent
- Frost-stable formula
- Now in Mint Glacier scent

Also repels bears! Made of environmentally friendly yeti pee, because even yetis are afraid of yetis.

APPENDIX A

THINGS NOT TO DO

1. Do not board the Luftzeug without an initiation charge.

2. Do not stare at non-humans.

3. Do not "joke" with I-MET. They take everything literally.

4. Do not touch an I-MET member.

5. Do not run from I-MET.

6. Do not converse with a poltergeist.

7. Do not remove, disable, or decorate your dormitory ghost trap.

8. Do not mis-shelve a book in the library.

9. Do not argue with Mrs. Spitz.

10. Do not mention sharp objects around Mrs. Spitz.

11. Do not use Aethereal dust.

12. Do not linger inside the Chattering Gazebo.

13. Do not attempt to pet, feed, or tame a yeti, bear, or tree.

14. Do not enter the President's gardens, residence, or observatory.

15. Do not enter a dark tunnel without a flashlight (or two).

16. Do not enter the White Forest alone.

17. Do not enter a new in-between.

18. Do not forget your in-between extraction technique.

19. Do not lose your soul.

This page
is not blank

APPENDIX B

GLOSSARY OF LETHAL BEASTS

Aethereal Mosquito (*Culicida aetherica*)

A mutation of the common mosquito observed in areas of elevated Aethereal energy. Larger, more aggressive, and unusually persistent, they feed with alarming efficiency and have been known to induce dizziness, hallucinations, and temporary paralysis in their victims. They do not respect DEET. Carry Indispensable™ Arctic Vampire Repellent.

Carnivorous Cottonwood (*Arbor vorax*)

Common and Man-Eating varieties of the White Forest. These trees remain temporarily rooted while sleeping. Most feature large jowls with very sharp and numerous teeth. All possess a flexible root system capable of dragging prey beneath the soil. They prefer non-Alaskan humans and are most active during daylight hours.

Earworm (Tunneling Variant) (*Vermis cerebrivorus*)

The stressed form of the otherwise harmless bookworm. Earworms burrow through soil and soft tissue with equal enthusiasm and are known to enter the human ear canal in search of cerebral tissue, which it devours. They are decidedly off-key hummers, who enjoy annoying jingles and thrive inside temporary in-betweens. Some can be rehabilitated.

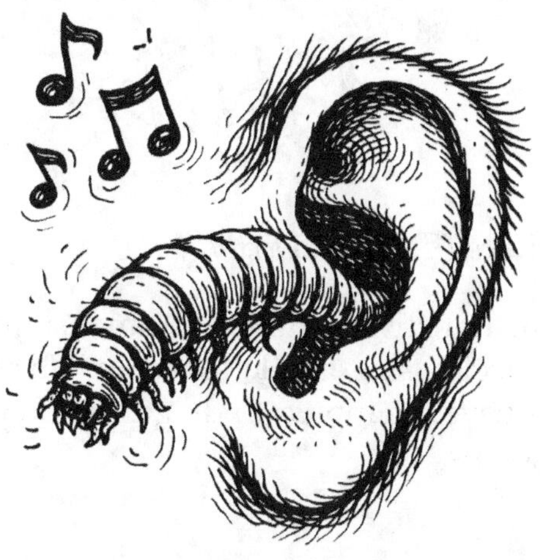

Frost Revenant* (*Homo gelidus redivivus*)

An animated corpse preserved by extreme cold and infused with Aethereal residue. These creatures wander during periods of high winds in winter and high temperatures in summer and are often mistaken for stranded hikers. Extremely strong, grumpy, and lacking higher brain function.

*I-MET has eliminated all known Frost Revenants in the greater BTU area. The last recorded sighting was by I-MET in 1972.

Hoarfrost Moth (*Noctua pruinae*)

A large, pale moth whose wings resemble frost crystals. Hoarfrost moths appear harmless until disturbed, at which point they release a cloud of freezing spores capable of causing cold-induced bronchospasm, frozen lung disease, suffocation, and death within minutes. Students should avoid breathing their spores.

In-Between Lurkers (*Tenebrae interstitii*)

A predatory organism native to unstable dimensional seams. These creatures vary in species, size, and lethal habit. They cannot survive long on Earth but have attempted to drag their prey through temporary in-betweens.

Mosquito (*Aedes communis*)

The common Alaskan mosquito is a summer hazard found in muskeg, forests, and poorly drained regions of campus. Though individually harmless, they can bite through clothes, and large swarms are capable of extracting enough blood to weaken even the hardiest hiker. Avoid Aerial Phlebotomy—use repellent with DEET.

Moss Stalker (*Muscoraptor sylvestris*)

A quadrupedal predator that mimics the appearance of White Forest moss and lichen. It lies motionless along trails until its prey steps close. Prefers non-humans and bunny rabbits. Presents no threat to humans.

Snow Howl (*Strix nivivox*)

An owl-like carnivore whose vocalizations can induce disorientation and hallucinations. Often works in cooperation with the Veilwolf.

Spruce, Carnivorous (*Picea sagittate*)

Similar in size and appetite to the Carnivorous Cottonwood. Stays green in winter. Can shoot its barbed 2-inch needles up to ten feet.

Tunnel Crawler (*Formica mortifera subterranea*)

A pale subterranean organism that looks and behaves much like a common fire ant, if fire ants had a deadly, anesthetizing bite. Inhabits BTU's dark tunnel system. One bite makes you tired. Two bites put you to sleep. Three bites put you in a coffin. Usually attracted to vibrations such as running and screaming. Repelled by light.

Veilwolf (*Lupus velarium***)**

A colossal White Forest predator of ancient origin whose appetite
extends beyond flesh to fear itself. Capable of slipping partially into
the Aether while hunting. Students report seeing only the creature's
eyes or teeth before an attack. Discouraged by good humor.

White Forest Yeti (*Gigantanthropus nivicola***)**

A massive omnivorous predator that prefers human meat
and avoids the nitrogenous waste of its own species. Carry
Indispensable™ Yeti Spray when traveling through the White
Forest.

WHITE FOREST
Olde Main
College of ParaScience
President's Residence
Edge Labs
IGLOO ARENA
"THE BOWL"
College of Geology
Trinity Center
Eureka Hall
Library
Hospital
College of Pre-Medicine
CIVILIZATION ROAD
Bear Towne University

STUDENT NOTES

There is literally NOTHING in Tunnel 7

You're blind

Holy Shit Stay away from 7!

THIS school is messed up

STUDENT NOTES

STUDENT NOTES

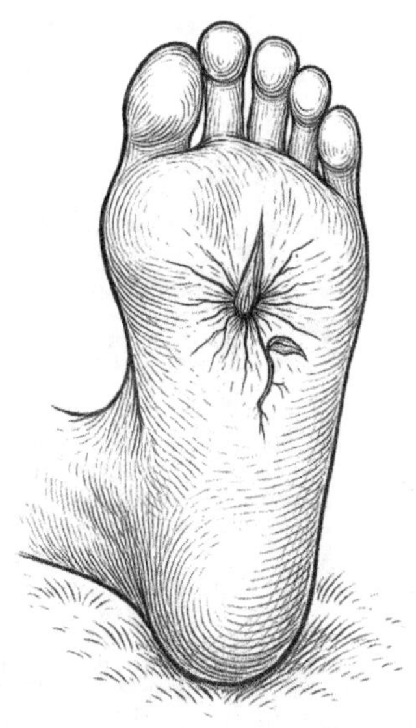

STUDENT NOTES